HER
IRRESISTIBLE
PROTECTOR

HER IRRESISTIBLE PROTECTOR

BY

MICHELLE DOUGLAS

MILLS
BOON

CAERPHILLY COUNTY BOROUGH COUNCIL	
3 8030 08257 4537	
Askews & Holts	06-Nov-2014
	£13.99
CCB356051	

® and ™ are trademarks owned and used by the trademark owner and/or its licensee. Trademarks marked with ® are registered with the United Kingdom Patent Office and/or the Office for Harmonization in the Internal Market and in other countries.

First published in Great Britain 2014 by Mills & Boon, an imprint of Harlequin (UK) Limited, Large Print edition 2014
Eton House, 18-24 Paradise Road,
Richmond, Surrey, TW9 1SR

© 2014 Michelle Douglas

ISBN: 978-0-263-24121-1

Printed and bound in Great Britain
by CPI Antony Rowe, Chippenham, Wiltshire

To my irresistible little sister, Jess.

CHAPTER ONE

'YES!' TASH FLUNG up the lid of the washing machine, bunched up a T-shirt and lobbed it into the dryer. A pair of shorts followed and then another T-shirt and a pair of tracksuit pants. 'Oh, yes, and she's going for the record...' A rolled-up sweatshirt sailed through the air and into the dryer without touching the sides. She grinned. As soon as she switched that baby on, her holiday officially started.

One glorious week.

Just to herself.

She did a little dance. A week! A whole week.

A knock on the front door pulled her up mid-shimmy and the next T-shirt sailed past the dryer to land in the laundry tub. She turned to glare.

No, no, don't glare. Holiday, remember?

She let out a breath, reaching for her customary languor and shrugged it on. As soon as she was out of Sydney she could carry on with as much uncool excitement as she pleased, but until then she had no intention of ruining her tough-customer image.

Chin tilted?

Check.

Swagger?

Check.

Bored facial expression?

Check.

At seventeen it had taken her weeks—months!—to perfect that particular attitude. Now she could slip it on at will.

She strode down the hallway, determined to get rid of whoever was on the other side as quickly as she could. Throwing open the door, she glanced at the figure outlined on the other side of the screen and everything slammed to a halt—her feet, her mind, her holiday mood. Screaming started up inside her head. Air pressed hard against her lungs—hot, dry and choking.

She swallowed to mute the screaming and folded her arms to hide the way her hands had started to shake from the surge of adrenaline that flooded her. Every stomach muscle she possessed—and her weekly Judo class ensured they were all well-honed—clenched up hard and tight until they hurt.

Mitch King.

Officer Mitchell King stared back at her like some upright holy warrior. From the top of his close-cut blond hair to the tips of his scrubbed-to-within-an-inch-of-their-lives boots. Even out of uniform he looked as if he should be wearing one. Everything about him shouted clean-cut hero—the strong square jaw, the not quite even teeth and the direct blue of his eyes. A man on a mission. A man who knew right from wrong. No shades of grey here, thank you very much.

Tash didn't reach out to unlatch the screen. She didn't break the silence.

'May I come in?' he finally asked.

She let her attitude prickle up around her like razor wire. Kinking an eyebrow, she leant one shoulder against the wall. 'Are you here to arrest me?'

His eyes narrowed. She knew their exact shade of blue, though the screen guarded her against their potency. Sort of. Her stomach clenched so hard she thought it might cramp.

'Of course not.'

'Then no, I don't think so.'

She started to close the door. He kept his voice even. 'It wasn't really a question, Tash. If you close the door in my face I'll break it down.'

She didn't doubt that for a single moment. As far as *Officer* Mitchell King was concerned, the ends always justified the means. For sheer cold-blooded ruthlessness, nobody else came close.

Without a word, she unclasped the door and then turned and hip-swayed down the corridor into the kitchen. She added the provocative sway to her hips because it was more dignified than thumbing her nose. And because without her usual uniform of jeans and work boots she felt vulnerable. A hip-sway distracted most men

Not that Mitch King was *most men*.

She turned, hands on hips, when she reached the kitchen, but the sun flooding in at the windows reminded her it was summer and that she had big plans for this week.

Just as soon as she got rid of her unwelcome visitor.

'How can I help you?'

The twist of his lips told her he'd read her animosity. As she'd meant him to. She'd lived in the same suburb as Mitch for most of her twenty-five years, but they hadn't spoken once in the last eight.

And if it'd been another eight it would've been too soon.

He didn't bother with pleasantries. 'We have a problem and I'm afraid you're not going to like the solution.' He planted his feet, but his eyes gentled. 'I can't tell you how sorry I am about that.'

He might look like an angel, but the man could probably deceive the devil himself.

She shook the thought off, refusing to allow soft summer eyes or firm lips that promised heaven to sway her. She wasn't seventeen years old anymore. 'I'm not interested in your sentiments.'

His mouth hardened.

'What's this problem? If it's anything to do with the pub then you'll have to speak to Clarke.'

'It's not about the pub.'

For the last three years Tash had managed the Royal Oak, a local establishment that serviced the factory workers in the area. It wasn't a genteel or trendy establishment by any means, but it was clean and generally free of trouble and Tash had every intention of making sure it stayed that way. She folded her arms and stuck out a hip. 'Well, if it isn't about the pub…?'

Mitch didn't even glance at her hip and she couldn't have said why, but it irked her. A tic did start up at the side of his jaw, though. He wasn't as calm as he'd like her to think.

'Have you spoken to Rick Bradford recently?'

It took every muscle she possessed to not let her jaw drop. When she was sure she had that under control she let rip with a short savage laugh. 'You have to be joking, right? The last time you and I spoke about Rick, you arrested him. Unfairly, I might add. If you think I'm going to chew the fat with you about Rick then you are an unmitigated idiot.' She put all the feeling she could into that *unmitigated*. It was a nice big word for a girl like her to know.

One of Mitch's hands clenched—a strong brown hand. He leaned in towards her, his eyes chips of ice, all warmth gone. 'So nothing's changed? You still see him through rose-coloured glasses?' His lip curled. 'What is it with women and bad boys?'

She lifted her chin. 'From memory, it wasn't the bad boy I fell for.'

He froze. He glanced away. So did she, wishing she could take the words back. It grew so silent the only sounds she was aware of were the low hum of the refrigerator and one of her neighbours starting up a lawnmower.

Mitch cleared his throat and from the corner of her eye she saw him reach into his pocket. He pulled out a packet of photographs and held them out towards her. 'We believe Rick is responsible for this.'

She didn't want to take the photographs. She wanted to slap his hand away, herd him back down the hallway and shove him out of her door. Mitch had always considered Rick a trouble-maker. When she and Rick had been in school, if anyone had been caught shoplifting then, according to Mitch, Rick must've been behind it. If there'd been a fight in the playground then Rick must've instigated it. If there was graffiti on the train station walls Rick must've put it there. She snorted. Crazy! And yet it had always been Rick's grandmother's door the police had come knocking on first.

And when kids in the area had been caught

smoking pot, Mitch had been convinced that Rick was the supplier.

Mitch had been wrong. Oh, so, wrong. But that hadn't stopped her best friend from going down for it all the same. He'd served fifteen months in prison. And she'd unwittingly helped put him there.

But not again. She'd learned some smarts in the last eight years. She knew better than to trust any man. Especially the one standing in front of her.

She reached out and took the photographs. The first one showed a house gutted by fire. She tossed it onto the counter. 'Rick is not, nor has he ever been, an arsonist.'

The second showed a crashed car. She glanced up and raised an eyebrow.

'The brake lines on the car were deliberately severed. The woman was lucky to get out of it with nothing but a broken collarbone and a concussion.'

She threw it to the bench to join its partner. 'Rick would never hurt a woman.' Rick protected women. She didn't bother saying that out loud, though. Mitch would never believe her.

The third and fourth photos made her stomach churn. 'And he certainly wouldn't senselessly slaughter animals. That's...' The photographs showed a field of sheep with their throats cut. One of them was a close-up. She slammed it face down to the bench. Acid burned her stomach. This was just another of Mitch's witch-hunts.

'That's what's happened to Rick's last three girlfriends.'

'I'm sorry, Officer King, but I'm afraid I can't help you with your enquiries.'

'Have you spoken to Rick recently?'

He'd rung her two nights ago to tell her he was coming to town.

'No.' She kept her face bland and unreadable. She'd practised and practised that skill until she had it down pat. 'I haven't spoken to Rick in months.'

His eyes narrowed. 'I'm not sure I believe you.'

She lifted a shoulder and let it drop. 'I don't care what you believe.' She paused and forced herself to complete an insolent survey of all six feet two inches of honed male flesh. Mitch still had a great body. She kinked an eyebrow when she met his gaze again, keeping her face bland.

'But it has to be said, you used a smoother approach last time.'

And, just like that, the air shimmered with unspoken tension. As if it hadn't been shimmering enough before!

'You're never going to forgive me, are you?'

'Nope.'

'I was trying to protect you.'

'Liar.'

She spoke so softly it almost sounded like an endearment. He took a step back, shrugged his official demeanour back on like a second skin. 'We have it on fairly good authority that Rick is headed for Sydney.'

She kept her mouth shut.

'And we think you're next on his hit list.'

It took an effort of will not to roll her eyes. 'Besides the fact that I know Rick would never hurt a woman—*any* woman—I've never been his girlfriend. I think that rules me out, don't you?'

'No.'

It was the way he said it. It made her blood run cold. Mitch might not make the law, but he sure as heck ensured it was enforced to the letter.

Regardless of the cost—to himself or to others. 'What makes you so sure I'm next on the hit list?'

'A crumpled-up piece of paper with your address on it.'

She went cold all over. 'Found where?'

'In that field of slaughtered sheep.'

She folded her arms, resisting the urge to chafe them instead.

'Two undercover officers from Central Sydney are on their way here now. One of them fits your description.'

We have a problem...you won't like the solution.

'And the bit I'm not going to like?'

'They're going to stake out your house to wait for Rick, and we have to get you out of here.'

She went to shake her head.

'For your own protection.'

It should've sounded ludicrously melodramatic, but it didn't. She stared at him for a long tension-fraught moment, taking in the way his mouth tightened and his shoulders tensed. '*We* meaning you?'

He nodded.

'This is a bit beneath you these days, isn't it?' He'd progressed through the ranks of the force with a speed that was apparently a credit to him and his family. She might call him Officer, but he was a detective now. She couldn't believe he hadn't moved to a flashier suburb and wiped the dust of this working-class neighbourhood from the soles of his polished boots. She couldn't believe he was standing in her kitchen asking her about Rick Bradford *again.*

She pointed to the suitcase on the sofa, open but neatly packed. 'Look, I'm about to head off on holiday for a week. Up the coast. I won't be around to spoil your stakeout or whatever it is you have planned.'

'You don't understand, Tash. We need to get you somewhere safe. We don't want to risk you ending up in hospital…or worse.'

'Why you?' The question burst from her, but she couldn't help it. She didn't want anything to do with this man. Ever. Again.

His nostrils flared. 'My history with Bradford is well known.' The words came out clipped and short. 'The powers that be want me out of the way.'

'So even your superiors think your judgement is clouded on the issue?'

He didn't say anything. He simply reached across and turned the photograph of the sheep over; spread each photograph out so she could experience their full impact.

She cut short a shudder. *Show no weakness.* Rick wasn't responsible for those dreadful things, but someone was. Someone who wanted to frame him or hurt him in some way. Someone who didn't care who they hurt in the process. She couldn't stop her gaze from flicking to the other photos—the burned-out house. How dreadful to lose all you owned in the world in one fell swoop. She glanced around her open-plan kitchen and living room. She didn't have much, but…

She glanced at the photo of the crumpled car and swallowed. Some of the questions Rick had asked her the other night made sudden and sinister sense—*Have any new people come to the area? Has anything unusual happened lately?* He'd asked them all in such a way that he hadn't raised her suspicions, but now…

She knew her rights. She could say no. For heaven's sake, she hadn't had a holiday *ever.* But she owed Rick. If she could help bring this situation to a swift conclusion—help clear him—

the sacrifice of a holiday would be a small price to pay.

'Where do you mean to take me?' She didn't doubt for a moment that Mitch had an ironclad plan.

He met her gaze and just shrugged.

Obviously it was a *secret* ironclad plan. 'How long do you think this operation is going to take?'

'No more than a few days.'

She glanced at the photographs again. Who on earth would want to hurt those women? And what did it all have to do with Rick?

A burned-out house. Severed brake lines. Slaughtered sheep. She suppressed a shiver. She might've learned some street smarts in the last few years, she might be known as someone not to mess with, but she had no desire to come face to face with whoever was responsible for all of that. She knew self-defence and she had a smart mouth, but this… It was out of her league.

Self-preservation battled with pride. Common sense eventually won out. She might hate Mitch, but not enough to endanger her own life. She could put up with him escorting her to wherever it was she needed to go. 'When do we have to leave?'

'Within the hour would be good.'

She bit back a sigh. 'You said there were two officers coming? I'll make up the bed in the spare room.'

'Just leave the linen out. They can make up their own beds.'

Typical male.

Her hand clenched. There was nothing typical about Mitch King, and she'd do well not to forget it. 'Then I guess I'll just throw the rest of the wet things in the dryer, pack a bag and get changed.'

'Tash, thank you.' She must've looked blank because he added, 'For being so reasonable about this.'

His gaze lowered to her fist. She unclenched it and pasted a fake smile to her face. 'I'm no longer an overwrought teenager, *Officer* King. I have absolutely no desire to meet the person responsible for those awful things.' She gestured to the photos. 'But I can tell you now, you're on the wrong trail if you think it's Rick.' And the sooner the police found that out the better.

He didn't say anything for a long moment. 'I

suppose it's too much to hope that you'll call me Mitch?'

'You suppose right.'

She stalked off, heart thumping.

'You already have a suitcase packed. You won't need to pack a separate bag.'

'They're holiday things.' Swimsuits and shorts and bright T-shirts. If she was lucky she still might get away for a couple of days.

'Which will all be fine,' he called after her.

That sounded promising. She wondered if the NSW Police Force budget extended to putting her up in a nice resort somewhere on the North Coast. It'd mean her week wouldn't be a complete loss.

She focused on that rather than the thought of spending the next few hours in Mitch's company.

She wasn't a teenager, she thought, lifting her chin. She was an adult woman with clear vision and hard-won wisdom. And she had Mitch's measure now.

Fool me once, shame on you. Fool me twice...

She shook her head. It wasn't going to happen.

After switching the dryer on she shot into her bedroom and pulled her mobile phone from her pocket, flicked through her list of stored numbers until she came to Rick's. She had to warn him of the welcome he could expect when he arrived in Sydney.

Mitch suddenly loomed in the doorway. Damn it! She hit delete and Rick's number disappeared.

His eyes could knife a lesser person. 'Were you trying to ring Bradford?'

'I'm ringing Mandy next door and leaving a message on her answer machine to tell her I'm letting some out of town friends stay. You know what this place is like. If strangers suddenly show up without explanation there'll be all sorts of alarms raised.'

He loomed in the doorway while she made the call. When she was done he held out his hand for the phone.

She lifted her chin and went to put it in her pocket instead.

'Don't test me on this, Tash.'

One glance at his face told her he'd take it by force if necessary. Steeling herself, she slapped it into his palm. 'I can see the next few hours are going to be a whole barrel-load of laughs. Now, I'd like some privacy while I get dressed.

Unless you mean to force your company on that head too.'

Without a word, he turned and stalked off. Tash had to sit down on the edge of her bed and breathe in for several long moments. She pushed herself upright again to pull on her usual armour of jeans, work boots and a black T-shirt.

It wasn't until they were driving over the Sydney Harbour Bridge with its comprehensive view of the Opera House and harbour that Tash realised how completely she drew Mitch's scent into her lungs. She stared out of the passenger window, barely noticing the colourful yachts below or the way the light glinted on the harbour in perfect summer exuberance.

Mitch's scent hadn't changed. Not one little bit. He still smelled of oranges and the tiniest hint of mint. Her lungs swelled to drink it in as if starved. With an abrupt movement she lowered the window, blasting her sinuses with warm summer air.

Mitch glanced at her briefly and she met his gaze just to prove she could. What she saw in their depths, though, shook her to her core. She understood the concern. She was a citizen at risk and he was the officer charged with protecting her. Her lips twisted. And she knew how seriously he took that duty.

But…regret?

Like him, she turned her gaze back to the front and tried to ignore the pounding of her heart.

'You will be safe, Tash, I promise. This will all be over before you know it.'

She believed him. Still, the sooner he dropped her off at the 'secret' location and went on his merry way the better.

Another ten minutes of bone-stretching tension crawled by.

'How is Rick doing?'

He spoke so softly she almost didn't hear him. She wished she hadn't.

Her fingers curved into talons. It took an effort of will not to bare her teeth at him like some wild thing. Eight years ago he'd taken from her not only her best friend, but also her self-esteem and her conviction that good trumped evil. She pushed a laugh out of her throat, but it was harsh and guttural. 'Do you really think I'm naïve enough to discuss him with you again? Or perhaps you think him stupid enough to discuss his comings and goings with me?'

His knuckles whitened about the steering wheel. She dragged her gaze back to the front. She remembered those hands more than she remembered his eyes or his smile. She remembered how he'd held her hand in his and the way his thumb had rubbed back and forth across her wrist, making her blood quicken, making her wish he'd do so much more with those hands. She remembered how one of his fingers had trailed down her cheek, and how it had made her feel like the most beautiful girl in the world. She remembered how his hands had curved about her face the couple of times he'd kissed her, as if she were precious.

Precious? She'd been nothing more than a means to an end.

She could almost forgive him for arresting Rick. He was a police officer and it was his duty to uphold the law. And once he'd seen what was happening, Rick had made sure all the evidence had pointed to him. Rick had taken the blame and had sworn her to silence. She couldn't blame Mitch for any of that. But she would never forgive him for using her to bring about that arrest, for lying to her, for betraying her so completely. For making her think he loved her. All in the line of duty.

'I only meant that I'd heard he'd been doing some good work with troubled youths down in Melbourne. That's a tough gig. I admire him for taking it on.'

Back then she'd been utterly clueless.

But not anymore. Seemingly innocuous questions or nicely worded flatteries would never draw her again. 'Well, maybe you'd like to make a donation to that cause the next time you have your chequebook open, *Officer* King.'

They didn't speak again. They drove along in a silence that itched and burned and bristled for another hour. Tash didn't say a word when he turned onto the freeway and headed north. He didn't volunteer any information either. Now there was a surprise.

Eventually he turned onto a small sealed road that wound effortlessly through bushland with only the odd farm dotted here and there to show any signs of habitation. Before they reached the road's end Mitch swung the car onto an obscured bush track.

'This isn't the way to a nice resort,' she growled.

'What on earth gave you the idea I was taking you to a resort?'

Her nose curled. 'Wishful thinking.'

He grinned and her heart sped up. Just like that. Idiot heart.

'Then where on earth are you taking me?' She made her voice tart. 'Or do we have to wait for a Cone of Silence to descend before that's to be revealed?'

'I'm taking you to a cabin.'

Her lip and nose curled this time. 'Please tell me it has running water and electricity.'

'It has both.'

How gullible did he think she was? 'I don't see any powerlines.'

'There's a generator.'

'Is there a flushing toilet?'

He flashed her a grimace pregnant with apology.

She huffed back in her seat and folded her arms. 'Why can't I go to a resort under an assumed name or something? I'll pay out of my own pocket.'

'It's not a question of money, Tash. It's a question of keeping you safe. The best way of doing that is to make you disappear, take you out of circulation.'

'You can't keep me here against my will.' Though they both knew that, if he chose to, he could.

'Do you really want to risk leaving?'

She glared out at the ghost gums and banksia trees.

He parked the car beneath a makeshift shelter that blended into the native Australian landscape. 'We have to walk the rest of the way.'

Oh, this was getting better and better.

He held his hands up at her glare. 'I swear it's only three minutes of easy walking.'

It would've been easy if it hadn't been for the bull ants. She yelped the moment she saw the first one.

Mitch spun around. 'What's wrong?'

She pointed.

'For heaven's sake, you're wearing work boots. They're not going to hurt you.'

'I hate them.' She'd sat on a nest of them once when she'd been small and she'd never forgotten it. They'd injected so much venom she'd developed a fever that night and had ended up in the emergency room of the local hospital. Her father had clouted her at the time for being so stupid as to sit on an ant nest. Then he'd clouted her when they'd got home from hospital for the additional inconvenience.

The memory made her stomach churn. She pushed a hand into the small of Mitch's back. 'Go faster.' He felt lean and hard beneath her fingertips. 'In fact, run.'

'Tash!' Exasperation laced his voice. He swung around to her, but whatever he saw in her face cut off the rest of his words. He knew she had demons. And she really hated him for that.

Thankfully, he didn't say a word. With a shake of his head he started to jog, her suitcase tucked easily under one of his arms as if it weighed nothing. She stayed close at his heels, her handbag bumping at her hip and her feet tingling in abhorrence at the thought of ants.

Mitch slowed to a walk when they emerged into

a clearing. Tash checked the ground for signs of bull ants before lifting her head. The clearing of lush grass opened up to a view so unexpectedly elemental and beautiful, so unspoilt, it momentarily robbed her of the ability to speak. She stumbled forward, her jaw sagging.

The curve of land they stood on caught an ocean breeze and below stretched a small beach. What the beach lacked in size it made up for in perfect golden glamour—the sand glittering in the sun and the waves whooshing up on the shore in perfect curls, the water stunningly clear and the whitecaps gloriously white. Beyond the bay the sea glimmered blue and green without a whitecap in sight.

To the left of them lounged a largish cabin, screened on its seaward side by wattle trees. The flowers were long gone, but the delicate green tracery moved in the breeze as if dancing to something slow and dreamy. Behind it stood a forest of ghost gums and banksia trees.

'Where…where are we?'

Mitch turned from unlocking the cabin's door. His mouth hooked up when he saw where she'd stopped. 'Pretty, isn't it?'

'Beautiful.' It might just make up for the rustic amenities. Suddenly, spending a few days in a secret cabin with a private beach didn't seem such a hardship after all.

She followed Mitch inside. She didn't bother trying to hide her relief.

He grinned. 'Not as bad as you were expecting?'

The main room, complete with a rug on the floor and a comfy-looking sofa against one wall, was warm and welcoming. To the left was a fully equipped kitchenette, with a microwave oven and bar fridge. A table with three mismatched chairs stood nearby and a solid wooden bookcase full of books and knick-knacks acted as a kind of divider between kitchen and living areas. There were even pictures on the wall.

He gestured to a doorway and Tash moved aside the blanket tacked to its frame to glance inside. It held a big double bed with a blue-and-white patchwork quilt. A white blanket box sat beneath the window. She shook her head, turning on the spot to take it all in. 'It's lovely. Truly lovely.' If she'd owned a cabin, this was exactly what she'd want it to look like. 'Who owns it?'

He glanced away. 'I do.'

Her jaw dropped. 'This is yours?'

'I bought the land five years ago.' He shrugged. 'I've spent my holidays and free weekends building this cabin.'

He'd what? For one outrageous moment she wanted to run away. Instead, she swallowed. 'Thank you for letting me use it.'

He didn't say anything.

She moistened suddenly parched lips. 'I guess you'd better show me the lavatory, and how the generator works. And then you can get back to cleaning up the streets and keeping the peace.'

Would he have to face whoever had hurt those women? Her heart surged against her ribs. She took a step back. She wouldn't want anyone to have to deal with someone that angry and unbalanced. Not even Mitch.

He frowned and cleared his throat. 'Tash, I think you've misunderstood the situation.'

She straightened from surveying the titles in the bookcase. Not that she'd taken in a single one of them. 'Oh?'

'I'm not leaving you here alone. I'm your body-guard for the duration of the operation.'

She dropped down onto the sofa. It really was very comfortable.

CHAPTER TWO

TASH'S EXPRESSION TOLD Mitch more than words could that she'd rather face whoever was responsible for hurting those women than spend any more time in his company.

He swung away, biting back a curse. They both knew the person responsible was Rick, and no doubt she still thought she could save him. Just as she'd thought eight years ago. He wasn't going to let that happen. He wasn't giving Rick the chance to hurt Tash again.

He waited for hysterics.

And kept right on waiting.

He should've known better. Tash didn't do hysterics. Not anymore.

Eventually he rolled his shoulders. She might never forgive him for putting Rick behind bars, but she was right—she wasn't the sweet, easily-rocked young girl she'd once been either. His heart bled a little at that, knowing he'd been partly responsible for that hardening, for her toughening up. He'd tried to apologise back then, but she hadn't wanted to listen. A part of him hadn't really blamed her.

He rubbed the back of his neck. Ancient history—that was all it was, and that was how it should stay. He pulled his hand back down to his side and bit back a sigh. It'd help if he didn't remember the events of eight years ago as if they'd only happened last week. His lips twisted. And how those events had changed his life forever.

For the better.

And for the worse.

'Is that really necessary—a bodyguard?'

He turned back and aimed for neutral and professional. He'd found that difficult eight years ago and he didn't find it any easier now. 'I don't make the rules, Tash. I just follow orders.'

'To the letter.'

He ignored her sarcasm. 'Naturally, you'll have the bedroom.' He gestured. 'I'll be on the couch.'

One quirk of her eyebrow told him that had never been in doubt.

A reluctant grin tugged at his lips. He had to

admire her spunk. 'Let's get a couple of things out of the way and then we can relax.'

'Relax? You really think that's going to happen?'

Her hazel eyes, a bit too large for her face, mocked him. They wielded the same power, the same kick of awareness now as they had eight years ago. When she'd been a slip of a girl and he'd been a hungry young constable eager for promotion. Seventeen. He'd had to keep reminding himself of that fact at the time.

She's not seventeen any more.

His chin shot up. He had no intention of letting his guard down while they were out here in the wild. None! He wouldn't relax until Bradford was in custody. There might be history between him and Tash, but he refused to be distracted by it. Or by her.

Besides, his lips twisted, she'd rather drink poison than become involved with him again.

It didn't mean he wasn't going to try and make this as easy on her as possible, though.

'What do we need to get out of the way?'

Her question hauled him back. 'First I'll show you the amenities.' The sooner she'd had a chance to rant about those the better.

She sighed when she saw the small outbuilding with its pan toilet and the bucketful of dirt and small spade beside it. 'At least it has a door.' She glanced in. 'And seems to be relatively spider-free.'

He remembered her reaction to the bull ants and made a mental note to make sure it remained spider-free. 'And this is the shower.' He gestured to the canvas hut nearby. A camp shower he'd only erected yesterday.

'Hot water?'

He shook his head. Her shoulders drooped a little and he had to fight the urge to swear. Tash might act tough—as if she could take on anything the world wanted to throw at her—but beneath it all he knew how vulnerable she was... and how gentle. If he found Rick first...

His hands clenched again. He would keep her safe. He swore that much.

No one would find them out here.

And the undercover detectives would deal with Rick with their usual efficiency. It suddenly occurred to him that he didn't envy them their job. Arresting Rick again would give him no satisfaction. Other than to know Tash was safe, that was.

Instead of a stake-out he got to spend the next few days in paradise with a beautiful woman. *Who hates your guts.* He planted his hands on his hips and glared up at the sky. *Professional, keep it professional.* It was all he had. In his bones he knew that as long as they stayed out here they'd be safe. All he had to do in the meantime was maintain his professionalism.

He turned back to find her surveying him with narrowed eyes. She pointed to the shower. 'When did you put that up?'

'Yesterday.'

'So you knew—' She broke off and folded her arms. 'No, you didn't.'

'I was spending a few days on leave out here.'

The brown flecks within the brilliant green of her irises gleamed like amber. He'd never seen eyes like them before.

'So I'm interrupting your leave.'

'It's no big deal.'

'Well, it only seems fair as you're interrupting my holiday,' she drawled. But the way she gripped her hands in front of her was at odds with the tone of her voice. The space between them filled with an edgy silence.

He cleared his throat. 'I'm impressed,' he managed, suddenly thirsting for an ice-cold beer and it wasn't even lunchtime. But her hair gleamed a dark rich brown and the sun bore down on his uncovered head. 'You don't seem too horrified by the amenities.'

She smiled. It was sudden and unconsciously sweet and it jammed his breath in his throat. 'I'm just thankful I don't have to relieve myself behind a bush. Rick and I would sometimes take off to the National Park for a couple of days and that was usually the case there.'

The moment the words left her mouth she looked as if she'd like to call them back.

He should change the subject, try and put her at her ease. But... 'You want to talk about it? Clear the air?'

She turned to face him fully. 'About Rick?' she said, obviously deciding not to misunderstand him.

'I know you hate me for arresting him.'

'I stopped hating you for that years ago, *Officer* King.'

That *Officer* set his teeth on edge. She wanted to bait him, wanted to prick and needle him. Normally he could shrug that kind of thing off. He tried to focus on the content of the conversation rather than the tone. 'If that's the case, then what's the problem?'

'The problem is I haven't forgiven you for using me to do it. I haven't forgiven you for pretending to be in love with me, for making me trust you, and then betraying me the way you did.'

The accusation in her eyes cut at him. His mouth filled with acid. She'd given her friendship to him freely and he'd abused it. 'Would it make a difference if I told you how sorry I am about that?'

'No. And frankly, Mitch, I don't want to talk about it. Let's just focus on getting through the next few days as easily and quickly as possible, all right?'

So that was what he could do with his olive branch, huh? Right. He nodded once and rolled his shoulders to try and ease the burn between them.

Tash tossed her head and tried to ignore the darkness in Mitch's eyes. She reached up behind to scratch between her shoulder blades. 'Is there anything else I need to know?'

He didn't smile. The shadows in his eyes didn't retreat. 'Don't go off on your own.' He gestured to the coastal forest that surrounded them.

She tried to get the expression in his eyes out of her mind. He wasn't some cute, roly-poly Labrador puppy she'd just kicked, but a grown man who'd screwed her over.

She puffed out a breath. She wanted—needed—him to keep his distance.

She scowled and glanced up into the never-ending blue of the sky. 'We're safe here, right?'

'Yes.'

'Some semi-deranged criminals aren't going to come crashing through the undergrowth, are they?'

He widened his stance. 'Practically guaranteed not to happen. Next to nobody knows about this place.'

'Right, then.' She dusted off her hands. 'I don't see why we can't carry on as we planned to before all of this nonsense.'

Three frown lines marred his forehead. 'I'm not catching your drift.'

'You'd planned on a few days R & R out here, right?'

'Right.' He drew the word out.

'Me, too. Well, not *here*, obviously, but I'd planned on spending a significant amount of this coming week on a beach.' She'd planned to travel five or six hours further up the coast, but…whatever. 'And for the rest of it I was planning to read a big fat novel or two, order takeaway pizza, eat too much chocolate and not do a scrap of work.'

After three years of working without a break, she deserved a holiday.

'You're suggesting we holiday together?'

'Not together!'

His lips twisted. 'Of course not. My mistake.'

'But…' If she wasn't going to worry herself into an early grave…'Yes, to the holiday bit.'

He shifted his weight again and it drew her attention to the long, clean lines of his legs. Her mouth dried. 'Except—' she suddenly pointed at him '—you're not to go strutting around without a stitch of clothing on like you probably do when you're here on your own. Skinny-dipping is prohibited.'

She shouldn't have thought of Mitch naked. A

whole host of illicit images pounded at her. Her cheeks started to burn. Very slowly a grin spread across his face. Eyes as warm as Mediterranean nights urged her to drop the attitude. Hands that, apparently, hadn't lost their allure for her over the past eight years tempted her to let down her guard. And the combined scent of mint and citrus curled around her, making her mouth water and an ache start up low in her belly.

Her chest cramped. Her pulse pounded. Her hands clenched.

His grin hooked up the right side of his mouth in the most intriguing way and her heart started to hammer. He leant in closer, swamping her with heat and mint and citrus. 'It'd be almost worth it just to see the look on your face. You might have a smart mouth and attitude to burn, Tash Buckley, but I have a feeling it'd be as easy as ever to unsettle you.'

It couldn't be possible! She fell back a step. She couldn't still want Mitch after all this time.

'Do it and I leave.' Fear made her voice tart.

He eased back and the tropical blue of his eyes hardened to chips of ice. 'Then you'd be a fool.'

Maybe, but at least she'd be a fool with her heart intact.

'We carry on exactly as we'd planned...*separately.*'

She turned and stalked back towards the cabin.

It was only for a couple of days, three at most, she told herself, storming into the bedroom where Mitch had deposited her suitcase. She flung it open and with as much speed as possible slipped into her swimming costume. All she had to do was keep things polite and pleasant. She might have to work at it, but...

Pleasant? She grimaced and pulled a shirtdress on over her head. Okay, pleasant might not be possible, but polite—distantly polite...very distantly—that should be manageable. For heaven's sake. The man was only doing his job. She owed him some measure of gratitude whether she liked it or not.

Okay, well, obviously she didn't like it, but she could be adult about this. She gritted her teeth. She would be adult about this.

She practised a smile. There wasn't a mirror in the bedroom to tell her how well she'd pulled it off. It felt plastic, but it had to be better than a snarl, right? She slipped her feet into flip-flops and sauntered back into the main room. Mitch sat at the table, just…

She swallowed. He just sat there.

She recalled his attempt to apologise.

She recalled the way she'd spurned it, threw it back in his face and her smile started to slip. With a Herculean effort she slotted it back into place. 'Mitch?'

He glanced up. He took in her bare legs and something flashed in his eyes. An answering tightness clenched her stomach.

She shook herself. 'I, um…' She frowned and leaned towards him. 'If I weren't here, what would you be doing?'

He shrugged. It seemed casual but something told her it wasn't. She swallowed and suspected her smile had become a grimace. 'Well, if I were you, I'd get on with it.'

Unless it was walking around naked or skinny-dipping.

'I suspect my being on the beach might cramp your style,' he drawled, his eyes hard in a way that didn't fit her memory of him.

He could be right. 'There's room enough for the both of us on your beach.'

'That's not the impression I got.'

She knew she'd been churlish, but… She tossed her head. Given their history, the least he deserved was churlish. He sure as heck couldn't imagine she'd be doing cartwheels about any of this.

She backed up a step. 'I'm going to go for that swim.' She didn't wait for him to answer, but shot straight out of the door and down the track that led to the beach.

The headlands on either side pushed straight out to sea, the weathered rocks grey and smooth. In a storm or high seas it would probably be dangerous to swim here, but on a clear easy day like today curling waves rolled up to shore, set after perfect set. It was the ideal surf for body boarding. Not that she had a body board. She'd have to content herself with body surfing instead.

She dropped her towel to the fine white-gold sand and, refusing to turn around and glance back behind her, set straight off for the water.

She paddled for a couple of moments, the shock of cold water tightening her skin. Lifting her face to the sun, she relished the contrast between the cold and the heat.

And then she surveyed the surf. She'd never swum at a deserted beach before. Even though she was a strong swimmer she preferred the safety of a patrolled beach. Today, though, knowing Mitch would undoubtedly be watching from some hidey-hole, she moved forwards into the water, greeting the waves and finally diving beneath one. She caught a couple of waves and in less than five minutes she gave herself up to the joy of being in the water.

And every time thoughts of Mitch or Rick and the threat to her wellbeing intruded, she pushed them right back out again.

She practised handstands until waves knocked her over. She caught waves until she was worn out. She floated, relishing the sense of weightlessness and the cool water enveloping her.

'Tash!'

The shout came from the shoreline. She started and gulped a mouthful of water, remembering in a rush that someone wished her ill. She turned to find Mitch waving her in.

Why?

Could this whole nightmare be over already?

With a queer twist in her abdomen, she headed for the shore. She took the towel he handed her. 'What's up?'

'You've been out there for an hour and a half. Don't you think it's time for a break?'

An hour and a half? She blotted moisture from her skin and tried to appear unfazed and unflustered.

She had nothing to be flustered about.

Except for the way Mitch's eyes kept flicking to her legs…and her hips.

He jerked away. 'And beyond time to top up the sunscreen.'

She squeezed water from her hair, towelled off as best she could and then pulled her dress back over her head. She did her absolute best to ignore him, but it wasn't easy when he paced a few short metres away, back and forth, back and forth, on those strong tanned legs of his.

She tore her gaze away to slap a sunhat to her head and spread her towel out. She collapsed on it and then pulled a tube of sunscreen from her bag. She reapplied it to her face, and then her arms and legs. She finally donned a pair of sunglasses.

He didn't say a word.

His silence irked her. 'Any news?'

He stopped pacing and shook his head. 'No news.' His face softened slightly. 'But I thought you might be hungry so I made lunch. Only sandwiches and fruit.'

She didn't want his face to soften when he looked at her! She didn't want her belly softening when she looked at him! She didn't want him looking out for her, bossing her around or telling her what to do!

'I don't need you doing things for me or telling me what to do. I'm capable of deciding when I need to put on sunscreen and I can make my own lunch!' The words rocked out of her with too much force.

He stiffened and his eyes flashed. 'I think you meant to say, "Thank you, Mitch, for going to the trouble".'

Ha! 'You, at least, are being paid to be here, being paid to make lunch, being paid to keep an eagle eye on me, while I'm supposed to just submit and say "Thank you, Mitch"?' She let fly with a loose laugh. 'As if that's going to happen.'

He threw the picnic basket to the sand. 'You want to quibble about money when your life is in danger?'

She hated the way her pulse leapt at his wide-legged stance and flashing eyes.

He wheeled away. 'If you think I'm going to keep taking this crap from you, Tash, you're sorely mistaken.'

He wheeled back and she leapt to her feet. 'What are you going to do about it,' she shot at him, slamming her hands to her hips. 'Throw me in a police cell?'

'The NSW Police Force is doing everything it can to keep you safe! Would it seriously hurt you to show some gratitude?'

'If it were any other officer here then there'd be no problem on that head. Get another officer down here today and I'll show all the gratitude you want!'

His face twisted and his voice rose. 'It's school holidays. Summer. There isn't another damn person available unless I call Peters in from her holiday *with her kids*. Is *that* what you want?'

She almost said yes, but in all conscience couldn't.

He slashed a hand through the air. 'Rick has timed this perfectly!'

It was as if he'd hurtled her back eight years—back to the confusion, the pain and the rage. The helplessness. The realisation of what she'd done. The realisation of what he'd done. 'Rick is innocent you block-headed idiot!' she screamed as loud as she could.

His eyes blazed like blue fire. 'You're the idiot—the *blind* idiot—where Rick is concerned.'

Every muscle bunched and tensed until she shook with it, frustration a murderous black bile in her blood. She not only knew how to disable, but how to make a person scream with pain while she did it. And she wanted to make Mitch howl. Her hands clenched and her temples pounded with such force she thought her head would explode.

She clenched a fist…raised it…

And then her father's image rose up in her mind and she went cold all over. She took a step back, her hand falling to her side, her chest rising and falling and burning. 'I have never loathed anyone in all my life with the intensity I hate you, Officer Mitchell King.'

He paled.

'I do not want to be here with you.' *She'd almost struck him!* 'What are my other options?'

'There's a safe house in Hornsby. You'd need to remain inside at all times, hidden.' He swung away, raked a hand back through his hair. 'I remembered how active you were—how much you hated being cooped up—and figured you'd prefer being out here.'

She swore and sat, rested her head in her hands for a bit. They couldn't go on like this. *She'd almost hit him!* The thought of being cooped up in a hot sweaty suburb didn't appeal one bit, though, either.

What on earth had happened to polite distance?

She lifted her head. She dragged in a breath. 'What kind of sandwiches did you make?'

'Ham and tomato.'

Her favourite. She reached into the basket and took one. 'Thank you.' But it came out stilted.

He sat then too, but he kept the basket between them. Wise. Very wise.

'I'm sorry.'

She didn't want an apology. She wanted him gone. *You can't have that. Get over it.*

'If I have this wrong and you'd prefer the safe house just say the word.'

She considered it. Seriously considered it. She stared at the beach, the surf, the sky. Eventually she shook her head. 'This,' she gestured to the beach, 'is better.'

A heavy silence descended.

Would you like to clear the air?

She set down her sandwich. Would it help?

Her chest cramped as she looked at him. 'Do you know I never trusted another man after what you did?'

He bowed as if buffeted by a sudden breeze. 'Tash.'

Her name groaned out of him and she didn't answer the incredulity in his voice. She couldn't.

He raked both hands back through his hair. 'Jesus, Tash, you were just a kid!'

She stiffened at that. 'What? You don't think a seventeen-year-old can truly love?' She'd loved him with her whole heart. She'd never felt as intensely, as passionately, as deeply about any man. Not before. Not since.

She never wanted to feel that way again. When she thought he'd returned her feelings she'd been on top of the world. When she'd found out he'd used her to gain information that had led to Rick's arrest…

Betrayed didn't begin to describe it. No amount of jubilation, not the highest of highs, was worth that kind of devastation.

He turned to her, his face grey. 'I'm sorry, truly sorry. I thought…I thought you'd get over it. I thought you'd treat it as a light flirtation. It wasn't until afterwards I realised how much I'd hurt you.'

'Light flirtation?' She stared at him in disbelief. 'Mitch, seventeen-year-old girls don't treat anything as light except, perhaps, parental rules.'

Which was why she'd sneaked out to meet Mitch that night. It was why she'd taken him to Cheryl's party. A party that had been raided as soon as Mitch's suspicions that cannabis was present were confirmed. Until that night she'd kept her 'romance' with Mitch a secret from everyone. Because he'd asked her to. Because it was the one bright thing she could hold onto when everything else around her was shabby and tacky. She hadn't wanted to let reality intrude.

In hindsight, what he'd been doing had become obvious, only she'd been too besotted at the time to see it, too distracted by the presents he'd brought her—chocolates, books and knick-knacks that she'd treasured. She'd been too awed by the attention he'd paid her, too thrilled by the desire in his eyes. Too consumed by the physical mayhem he'd created in her.

She'd been altogether too stupid, too gullible and too naïve. But she'd learned her lesson— trust no one.

'I was twenty-two and I thought I knew every-thing.' He gave a laugh that scraped her nerve-endings raw.

Twenty-two? He'd seemed like a god to her back then. She'd forgotten how young he'd been too.

'But I got a lot of things wrong, Tash.'

She wouldn't argue with that, but something in his tone had her swinging to him. 'Like?' The question was out before she knew it.

He stared down at his hands and then out at

the water. He didn't wear sunglasses to shade his eyes and she could see the lines fanning out from their corners. He must be what—thirty, now? He was too young for so many lines.

And just like that her heart started to burn for him.

She stiffened and took another bite of her sandwich. She wasn't forgiving him.

'When I first started in the police force I was hungry to save the world.' His lips twisted. 'You can translate that into hungry for promotion if you like.'

'Which is why nailing Rick on drug charges was such a coup for you.'

He nodded.

Hungry to save the world? She scowled at the water. He hadn't saved. He'd only destroyed. The sad thing was, he didn't know just how much he'd destroyed. And even now she couldn't tell him. Wouldn't tell him.

'So you must be pleased with yourself these days.' She rested back on one hand as if she didn't have a care in the world. As if they were talking about nothing more innocuous than the weather.

'Moving up through the ranks as you have with such commendable speed.'

'You'd think so.'

She frowned and moistened her lips.

'But I got *you* wrong, Tash. I misjudged what I'd need to do, what I'd need to sacrifice, to rise up through the ranks and make a difference. I don't know if you remember this, but the day Rick was found guilty and was sentenced you turned to me with such a look in your eyes.'

The look had been heartbreak. Her eyes burned. 'It didn't stop you then and it hasn't stopped you now.' And she'd best not forget that.

He was quiet for a long moment. 'Some things are worth fighting for. I happen to think the law and justice are two of those things.'

'And if someone gets hurt in the crossfire?'

'In the interests of the greater good then...' He hesitated. 'I won't pretend that I don't regret it.'

The innate ruthlessness chilled her.

A seagull landed nearby. It squawked at them, obviously hoping they'd throw some scraps. She went to toss it her crust but Mitch's hand on her arm stopped her. She froze beneath his touch.

'It's cruel to feed them. Their digestive systems

aren't designed to eat bread…or chips,' he added, referring to the tourist habit of tossing gulls hot salted chips.

She nodded and he removed his hand and she found she could breathe again, although her heart pounded harder than the occasion demanded. 'Why on earth did you want to be a policeman anyway?'

His face darkened. He stared out to sea. 'I haven't told anyone this before. But if anyone deserves to know it's you.'

He turned and she may as well have not been wearing sunglasses at all. Her breath became trapped by the lump in her throat. The lump stretched into a painful burn that made her eyes sting. And all she could remember was the way his hands had cupped her face eight years ago and how utterly she'd given her heart to him.

'No,' she croaked.

He frowned. 'No?'

Clear the air? She gave a harsh laugh that made his nostrils flare. Clearing the air wasn't helping at all. This wasn't clearing anything, only clouding it.

'No,' she repeated, clearing her throat so the

word emerged stronger. 'I don't want to know anything more about you, Officer King. You can keep your secrets to yourself.'

With that she rose, shook out her towel and strode off towards the cabin. She entered it only to find him two paces behind. She whirled on him. 'Are you going to dog my every footstep?'

He stepped around her, seized a bottle of water from the fridge and grabbed the backpack from the table. 'Help yourself to whatever you want, Ms Buckley.' He waved a hand around the kitchen. 'I'll be down on the beach if you need anything.'

The 'Ms Buckley' stung, but she had no one to blame but herself.

She hitched up her chin. 'Thank you.' Her voice came out cold, polite and distant. If she'd had any energy to spare she'd have applauded her poise.

Without another word, he left.

She clenched her eyes shut. Letting her guard down around Mitch would be fatal. He might come across all caring and solicitous, but he didn't trust her any more now than he had back then. That backpack being a case in point. He'd been *very* careful to take it with him. She'd bet her life it contained her cell phone. And his. Along with the car keys. He wasn't giving her a chance to get her hands on any of them.

'Regret? Yeah, right,' she muttered. Mitch would say anything and do anything to get what he wanted. All in the line of duty, of course.

Well, one thing was for certain. He wasn't getting her.

Tash had a shower.

She fully explored the inside of the cabin. It was well-stocked. She had to give Mitch credit for that. She didn't find her cell phone. Not that she expected to.

She lay on the bed and stared up at the ceiling. Despite all the sun and surf earlier, a nap eluded her. Her mind circled with questions and fears instead. What kind of trouble was Rick in? Was he safe? Who was behind the violence against those women? Did someone really want to hurt her? If so, why?

She leapt off the bed to browse the bookcase. She selected a book at random. Fifteen minutes later she threw it down with a growl. The one thing she didn't need to read was a graphic police procedural.

Not that she was scared. Not out here.

Not with Mitch so close.

The thought whispered through her. She shook it away.

She made tea and drank it without tasting a single drop.

Finally she pulled on her tennis shoes, grabbed an apple and headed back down to the beach. Activity—that was what she needed. She wasn't used to lazing around with nothing to do.

The minute Mitch saw her he snapped his cell phone shut with a curt, 'I've got to go.' He shoved it into the backpack.

He didn't tell her who he'd been talking to.

She didn't ask.

'If it's *legal*,' she drawled, channelling icy politeness that bordered on incivility, 'I was planning to go for a walk…just along the shoreline.' She wanted to add 'Alone' but figured that'd be overkill.

'Sure.' He lay back on the sand and adjusted his cap over his eyes. 'Beyond those rocks there—'

he waved to the left '—is a broad rock shelf. The rock pools are pretty at low tide.'

Right. Was it low tide now? 'Thanks.' Again—icy and uncivil. It had to be better than shouting at him, though, surely? With a shake of her head, she turned and stalked off.

For the next hour Tash lost herself in the strange wonder of the rock pools. She discovered brightly coloured anemones, tiny starfish, small crabs and little silver fish. She found brightly coloured pebbles, and bright green clumps of seaweed. She found fully contained worlds that seemed to be in perfect harmony.

She grimaced as a hermit crab pounced and devoured a tiny fish. It was a beautiful world, but a savage one too.

Still, with the sounds of the waves breaking on the reef, the cries of the seagulls and the tang of salt on the air mixing with the scents of the eucalypts and casuarinas onshore, it worked to ease some of the tension from her muscles.

Until the image of Mitch's shuttered face rose up in her mind.

Had she really cut him off so pitilessly and walked away when he'd been about to reveal something that obviously meant a lot to him, some secret he'd never shared before? She slammed her hands to her hips. She glanced first one way then another before crouching back down.

'What a cow!' she murmured, scratching her hands back through her hair and knocking off her hat. She snatched it back up, settled it more firmly on her head. She was better off not knowing his secrets and he'd be better off not sharing them with her.

She thumped down to sit on hard rock. How were they going to get through three more days of this? Her mouth went dry. For heaven's sake she'd nearly hit him. They couldn't go on like this.

She forced steel to her legs and pushed back to her feet, startling the tiny fish in the rock pool. They flashed silver as they scattered to hide in the weed and overhangs. *For heaven's sake, it was eight years ago. Get over it!*

She passed a hand over her eyes. She hadn't spent the last eight years nursing her wound. But…seeing him when she'd least expected to had brought it all rushing back—the pain, the disillusion, the anger. Nothing good had come from any of it. All she'd been able to do was lash out in an effort to protect herself. *Very adult of you, Tash.*

She closed her eyes and lifted her face to the sun. She stayed like that, motionless, for several long moments. Swallowing, she turned and headed back the way she'd come.

Mitch still lay on his back with his cap over his eyes. She set her shoulders and went to nudge him with a foot and then thought the better of it. 'Are you asleep?' she murmured instead. She said it quietly so he could ignore her if he wanted.

'Nope.'

But he didn't sit up.

She sat, but not too close. 'I have a proposition for you.'

He still didn't sit up. In fact, he didn't say anything at all. She refused to get passive aggressive. She refused to get up and stalk off. 'The police want to question Rick, right?'

He hadn't been moving before, but he stilled completely at her words. She stared at him and pursed her lips. *Act like an adult.* 'I'd rather have this conversation face to face.'

* * *

Very slowly Mitch pushed up into a sitting position. What was she up to now? He settled his cap back onto his head. 'You know we do.'

'But you don't have enough evidence to arrest him, do you? All of your so-called evidence is merely circumstantial.'

'What are you getting at, Tash?' He reached across and removed her sunglasses, dropping them to her lap. He wanted to see her eyes. He wanted to know if she was lying to him, if she was planning something stupid. Not that she was the easy-to-read girl she'd once been, but he'd become adept at reading people. You had to in this job.

Her face, however, gave nothing away. She merely blinked a couple of times while her eyes adjusted to the light.

'If you think for one moment I'll believe you mean to grass Rick up or set him up, then you can think again.'

She leaned back and stared down her nose at him. 'I might consider you a treacherous snake in the grass but I never thought of you as stupid. Of course I'm not going to grass Rick up.'

She said it all so matter-of-factly and without rancour that it surprised a laugh out of him.

'I know Rick isn't responsible for these crimes you're fingering him for.'

All of his mirth fled. She was so blind where Bradford was concerned.

'Let me ring him. Let me speak to him.'

He stiffened. Every muscle screamed *no*. If he said no outright, though, she'd get up and walk away. He didn't want her to walk away. He was tired of that cold shoulder of hers.

His lips twisted. So much for professionalism.

Her hazel eyes with their bright points of gold surveyed him steadily. He bit back a curse. 'Why would I let you do that? Why would I give you the opportunity to warn him we're on his tail?'

She leaned towards him and the shape of her lips held him momentarily spellbound. 'Whatever happened to innocent until proven guilty?'

'I know Bradford.'

'You always had it in for him—why?'

'He was a drug runner!'

'You had it in for him well before that. For what? Shoplifting a couple of chocolate bars and a bit of petty vandalism? For heaven's sake,

Mitch, those things were a rite of passage where we grew up. You know that as well as I do. I'm guilty of exactly the same things!'

He clenched his teeth so hard he could feel the pulse at the base of his jaw start to thump. Eventually he managed to unclench them. 'He was the ringleader who led kids like you and Cheryl O'Hara astray.'

'Cheryl?' She closed her eyes. When she opened them again her eyes had turned dark and murky. 'You're wrong. You don't know how wrong.'

Her certainty made something inside him snap. 'I know he hit you all right!' The words burst from him like bullets—hard, sharp and lethal. His hands clenched. His gut clenched. Bradford had hit her and the knowledge still made him want to tear the guy apart with his bare hands. How could she still defend him after all this time? 'I know that mongrel beat you up!'

Her back stiffened. 'He most certainly did not!'

Her hauteur gave him pause, but not for long. He stabbed a finger at her. 'The first time I saw you after my basic training, you had a bruise on your cheek. A couple of months later, you had a black eye.' One incident could be shrugged off as an accident. But two? Not a chance.

Tash folded her arms.

'You had a black eye and Rick had two black eyes, a broken nose and a cut lip.'

She lifted her chin.

'I asked your father about it. He told me Rick had hit you and that he'd, um…taken Rick to task for it.'

'And you believed him?'

He sensed the scorn deep inside her. It burned brighter and fiercer until her eyes almost turned green. 'Of course I believed him!'

The scorn flared with greater intent. 'Of course you did.'

She went to rise, but he caught hold of her wrist, keeping her in place. 'Are you telling me Rick didn't hit you?'

With surprising agility she twisted out of his grip and it suddenly occurred to him that she only remained where she was because she chose to. 'Of course he never hit me!'

'Then who…?'

She raised an eyebrow, not even trying to hide

her derision. 'You're the detective, you work it out!'

Mitch watched her stalk back up to the cabin. When she was out of earshot, he let loose with a whole litany of curses. What on earth had possessed him to bring her here? What had made him think it a good idea? Why had he thought this would work?

He fell back to the sand to stare at the sky. All he wanted to do was keep her safe!

Of course he never hit me!

He sat back up with a frown. Her voice, her face, her eyes, they'd all conveyed too much authenticity. He wiped his palms down his board shorts. If Rick hadn't hit her then who the hell had?

His skin turned clammy. His mouth dried. A sheen of ice froze his scalp. No. Please God. He couldn't have gotten it so wrong!

He launched himself upright and sped towards the cabin. He flung the door open and didn't bother closing it. Tash spun around from washing her hands in the sink.

'Your father,' he croaked. 'Was it your father who hit you?'

She folded her arms and glared. 'Well you saw how handy he was with his fists.'

Not a direct answer, but he saw the truth in her eyes. His stomach pitched and he had to swallow to battle nausea. How could he have gotten it so wrong? All this time... 'Why didn't you tell me?'

Her lips twisted as if he were the most pathetic thing she'd ever seen. 'You never asked.'

Every word found its mark, knifing through him in accusation.

'My father was a big man. You saw the results of his handiwork.'

He had. He dragged a hand down his face. 'Rick tried to stop him?' From hitting her?

Again she didn't answer, but something bitter and broken stretched through her eyes. 'And you decided to do nothing about it.'

A fist tightened vice-like about his chest. Tash was right. He'd chosen to do nothing, believing Rick had come by his just deserts. Oh, he'd taken Mr Buckley to task and told him to never take the law into his own hands again, but...

He'd gotten it wrong. So wrong.

She twisted the knife in deeper. 'If you'd tried to befriend Rick instead of hassling him at every turn, you might've been able to help. He had enough misery in his life without you adding to it.'

She stalked past him and into the bedroom, and this time he didn't try to stop her.

CHAPTER THREE

MITCH STUMBLED BACK OUTSIDE. The bright light half-blinded him, but it was the light of new knowledge that made him reel.

How had he read her situation so wrong back then?

He wove his way back down to the beach—to where he'd left the backpack and his beach towel. He'd been twenty-two and so sure he knew everything. He'd known nothing!

He raked both hands back through his hair and let forth a curse that turned the air blue. How much had he contributed to Rick's spiral into crime? If he'd taken the youth under his wing could he have…?

A growl burst from the back of his throat. Rick would've resisted any overture of friendship from him. Rick hadn't trusted anyone in a position of authority. One of the few delights Rick had enjoyed, as far as Mitch had been able to tell, was flouting authority with a casual insolence designed to set teeth on edge, breaking rules wherever possible and laughing in the face of the consequences.

Given the boy's home life, Mitch could hardly blame him for his anger and lack of trust. Even when that anger had found a voice in petty crime. But as soon as Rick had progressed to drugs he'd stepped over an invisible line. Mitch glared out at the horizon. He refused to take responsibility for that.

But it didn't change the fact that he and Rick had more in common than he'd thought—they both loathed violence against women. At least, Rick had before he'd gone to jail.

Mitch rested his hands on his knees, pulled in a breath and let it out slowly before straightening. It might not be the case anymore. Prison changed a man, and from all he'd heard Bradford hadn't been a model prisoner.

He thought back to those photographs and his stomach hardened. Prison could send men who were on the brink right over it. The Central Sydney detectives in charge of the case thought him *guilty as sin*. Those were Detective Glastonbury's exact words. Mitch had no reason to doubt them. Rick mightn't have been responsible for hurting Tash eight years ago, but he was responsible for this latest spate of violence. Mitch was sure of it, even if Tash couldn't see it.

Just like you were sure he'd hit Tash eight years ago?

He swung away. It wasn't just Rick's connection to the three women. There was compelling physical evidence too. The evidence *wasn't* just circumstantial. Ice tiptoed down each of his vertebrae. He would not give Rick the chance to hurt a fourth victim. His lips thinned. Bradford must have a heck of a grudge against Tash—might even hold her responsible for his going to jail. That would make him dangerous. Savage.

He pushed his shoulders back, his nostrils flaring. Tash's protector had become a predator.

Teenage girls don't take anything lightly.

Rick had stood up to her father, had tried to take him on. Mitch's heart pounded against the walls of his chest. No wonder she had him up on a pedestal. No wonder she refused to listen to reason now. This would all eventually lead to more disillusionment on her part and she didn't deserve that.

He bit back a curse, swept up his towel, back-pack and sunglasses and marched back towards the cabin.

Tash wasn't in the main room, which meant she must be in the bedroom. He stared at the blanket he'd tacked to the doorframe in an attempt to give her a measure of privacy. 'Tash?'

No answer.

He threw his towel on the back of a chair, lowered the backpack onto it and tossed his glasses to the table with so much force they slid off the other side. Biting back a curse, he picked them up and slammed them back to the table.

'Tash, I want to talk to you!'

His words emerged at a bellow. He grimaced. Wrong tack. Totally wrong tack. He closed his eyes and counted to five. He opened them, counselling himself to moderate his tone. 'I want you to tell me about this proposition of yours. Why should I let you ring Rick?'

Finally the blanket was pushed aside as if she'd been standing on the other side the entire time, waiting for the right moment to make an entrance. 'Do you mean to give my idea a fair hearing?'

Her scepticism stung. 'I'm not making any promises. The ultimate decision rests with the detective in charge, not me. But if your idea has merit then I'll put it forward.'

He waited for some crack about him always following the rules or something, but she remained silent. 'Why?' she eventually asked, not moving from the doorway.

She acted as if he were the predator rather than Rick. He tried to relax.

'I mean I could tell down at the beach that you didn't like the idea.'

He'd grown better at reading people, but so had she. It'd be wise not to forget that.

She folded her arms. 'Well?'

His chin rose. 'I'm sorry I got things wrong eight years ago. I'm sorry I jumped to conclusions and didn't ask the right questions.'

She glanced away.

Mitch hardened his heart. 'You might not want to hear my apology, but that's not going to stop me from uttering it. I *am* sorry. You might not want to accept that, but that's your problem.'

'Problem?' she spluttered, her eyes glaring back into his.

'What else would you call that chip on your shoulder?'

Her eyes narrowed.

'But I'm through with apologising now. I'm sorry I got some things wrong back then. I'm sorry I hurt you. Now, you've made it abundantly clear that you don't want to be friends. Fine. So let's dispense with the pretence and keep everything on a professional footing.'

She blinked.

'Eight years ago I made a mistake. If I can in some measure rectify that now then I will.'

She finally moved further into the room, letting the blanket drop behind her. 'Are you saying you believe Rick is innocent?'

'That's not what I'm saying.'

Her lips tightened, but she didn't turn and stalk back into the bedroom. Instead, she strode to the fridge, pulled out a jug of iced water and snagged a couple of glasses from the kitchen bench. She sat at the table—in the seat nearest the backpack, as if to deliberately taunt him. He had to bite back a grin. They both knew she hadn't a hope of getting more than three steps away with it if she tried.

She poured them both a glass of water. 'The police want to question Rick, right?'

He sat too and curled a hand around his glass, relishing its coolness. 'That's right.'

'Do you actually want to arrest him?'

He wasn't telling her that but, man, she could keep her face smooth and unreadable these days. 'We'll want to hold him for questioning.'

'So, in the interest of achieving that, you're staking out my house whilst providing me with a bodyguard for what—three days? Does that seem like a reasonable use of police time and resources?'

'We take violence against women very seriously.'

She went on as if he hadn't spoken. 'When I believe that with a single phone call I could convince Rick to walk into the nearest police station.'

He leaned across the table. 'To give himself up?'

She glared. 'To *assist* with your enquiries,' she

snapped. 'I hope whoever *questions* Rick is more open-minded than you are, Officer King.'

He gulped water down to drown the immediate response that surged to his lips. 'Why would Rick do that?'

She ran a finger through the condensation forming on her glass. 'Because, against all the odds, Rick still trusts me.'

That was just what Bradford wanted her to think while he lulled her into a false sense of security. 'And you expect me to believe you'll just hand him in?' What was her game?

Her eyes flashed fire and he waited for her to start yelling at him all over again. She didn't, but the fire didn't dim. He had an unbidden image of her naked with that kind of fire glowing in her eyes. Would they—?

He tried to wipe his mind clear of the images that flung themselves at him in vivid succession.

'We're working on two different premises here.'

He hauled himself back to the present and this moment.

'You're operating under the mistaken illusion that Rick is guilty. I'm operating under the correct assumption that he's innocent.'

'If he's so innocent, Tash, why hasn't he already contacted the police?'

'What if he's not even aware of these crimes yet?'

He hated to shatter her illusions but the sooner she faced up to the reality the safer she'd be. 'Physical evidence linking him with the crime scenes has been found. We know he's recently been in the houses of each of the victims.'

She sucked her bottom lip into her mouth.

'He knows, Tash.' He resisted adding *he's guilty as sin*, even as he thought it. Her eyes flashed again anyway.

'Were his fingerprints found on a can of kerosene that could've been used to start the fire, or on a knife that might've been used to slit those sheep's throats or on the car that crashed?'

'No, but—'

'But nothing!' She dismissed his words with a slash of her hand.

'Despite what I've just said, you still believe he knows nothing about these crimes?' It took all of his strength to remain at the table like a civilised person, instead of overturning it like a mad man.

'No.'

The air was punched out of him.

'If he's been to see these women recently then he's bound to know about the crimes.' Her lips tightened. 'But Rick has no reason to trust the police. Maybe he's trying to find some hard and fast evidence first. Maybe he's trying to solve the crime himself.'

He could see how she could make that leap into her own mind, but he wasn't buying into it. 'Who do you think is responsible then?'

The fire in her eyes dimmed. 'I don't know. My best bet would be someone he was in jail with. Someone he made an enemy of. Someone who wants to get back at him.'

He clamped down on his tongue for three seconds before releasing it. 'Why would talking to you change his mind about going to the police?'

'Like I said, he trusts me. If he's innocent, as I believe he is, then he doesn't really have anything to fear. Other than how long it will take you lot to find out who's really responsible.'

He mulled that over for a moment.

'And if it brings a quick resolution to this mess then surely it's worth it.'

She had a point, but… He caught her gaze and

held it. 'How do I know that you won't simply warn him about the stake-out?'

Her gaze didn't waver but a certain satisfaction spread across her face. 'You don't. You'll simply have to trust me, Officer King.'

She practically purred his name. It was all he could do not to reach across and kiss her.

Tash held her breath and waited to see what decision Mitch would come to. The sooner this farce was over—the sooner she was away from Mitch—the better.

But it's not a farce, a tiny voice whispered through her.

No, not a farce. Someone really was out there hurting women. And she was next on this madman's list. Her skin iced over.

She planted her hands on the table. 'Mitch?'

He glanced up, his eyes widening at her use of his name instead of the sarcastic *Officer King*. 'You seem to forget that I have a personal stake in making sure the correct criminal is caught.'

She had absolutely no desire whatsoever to meet this person—whoever he was—face to face. She thought of those sheep, of that crumpled car and that burned-out shell of a house and had to suppress a shiver.

He reached out as if to take her hand, but his hand fell short. The blood pounded through her. 'I haven't forgotten that for a single moment.'

She believed him. Despite their history—or maybe even because of it—he would do everything in his power to keep her safe.

'Then surely my suggestion is worth considering?'

Eventually he nodded. 'You're right.'

She sat up straighter. 'Really?'

'Can you pass the backpack over?'

She did.

Her heart dipped, though, when he pulled his phone from the bag rather than hers. Of course he'd run this by his superiors first. In fact, this whole show of openness could just be a front to win her over.

Not going to happen.

What guarantee did she have that he'd argue her case sufficiently?

None.

You'll have to trust him.

That wasn't going to happen either.

'Detective Glastonbury, it's Detective King here.'

She snapped to attention.

'No, no trouble and no sightings from our end either.'

She listened as he outlined her proposition. Some of the tension trickled out of her when she realised he was arguing her case with creditable conviction.

'I believe she's trustworthy.'

She blinked. Did he mean her?

'But—'

She glanced up but, other than recognising that he listened intently, she couldn't make out anything else from his expression. Eventually he nodded and said, 'I understand.'

Her heart dipped. He rang off and her nose curled. 'They didn't go for it. I'm sorry.'

Was he? She shrugged. 'What was their beef?'

'Besides the fact that they believe they're tightening the net about him and will have him soon anyway?'

She heaved back a sigh. 'They didn't want to take the risk that I might tip him off.'

He hesitated.

'Out with it.'

'They seized his phone records.'

She gazed back at him blankly.

'Tash, they know you spoke to him on Thursday night for over ten minutes.'

Oh.

'You lied about that.'

Yeah, she had. There didn't seem to be much to say after that. Except… 'If they have his phone records then surely they can trace where he is by his mobile phone signal?'

'They did. His phone had been dumped in a garbage can in a shopping centre.'

Right.

'You want to tell me what you and Rick spoke about?'

'Nope.'

'You're not doing yourself any favours.'

'If he doesn't have his phone my plan wouldn't have worked anyway.'

His gaze never left her face and it took all of her willpower to not fidget under it. She shrugged again. 'Besides, I can tell you that we just shot the breeze together until I'm blue in the face, but you still won't believe me.'

His lips twisted into a sort of half-grimace, half-rueful smile. She stared at that mouth and remembered how it had felt against hers. So long ago. Would it feel the same now?

'I guess the point is moot. In a couple of days Rick will be in custody and enquiries will be underway.'

His voice dragged her back. She tried to shake herself free from the fascination gripping her. She and Mitch were obviously stuck out here for the duration and she'd have to learn to deal with it. But...

She sank back in her chair. What were they going to do for the next three days? Swim, soak up some rays, read a book or two?

She was honest enough to admit she might find some distraction in the swimming, but she wouldn't be able to relax enough to savour anything sedentary.

She bit back a sigh. 'Well, thank you for at least running my idea past the powers-that-be.' She sipped her water, circling a finger through the watermark it had left on the table. 'And thank you for arguing my case. You didn't have to do that.'

He rose and stowed the mobile phone into the

backpack and then dropped the bag to the floor near the wall. He didn't sit again. 'You didn't think I would?'

She moistened her lips and shook her head. He hadn't thought her idea a good one in the first place.

'Careful, Tash; you're letting your resentment cloud your perception. It would probably be wiser to judge me on who I am now rather than who I was eight years ago.'

That had an uncanny ring of truth to it and it almost raised her hackles. She forced them back down. She was tired of sniping at him. She needed to deal with this situation like an adult.

He glanced at his wristwatch. 'Time to get dinner on.'

She blinked. She opened her mouth. She closed it again.

He kinked an eyebrow. 'What?'

'You can cook?'

'Of course I can cook,' he said incredulously. 'It's not rocket science.' He went to the fridge and removed a tray of minced meat. 'Just because I'm male doesn't mean I'm useless in the kitchen.'

She kept her mouth firmly zipped.

'So I'd appreciate it if you'd keep your sexist views to yourself.'

That was almost enough to make her unzip it.

He stilled and then turned to her, a couple of fresh tomatoes and a jar of tomato paste in his hands. 'You were being sexist, right?'

She considered drawling, *Absolutely*, and leaving it at that, but the word wouldn't come.

'You weren't?' His shoulders relaxed. 'Sorry; I thought…' He shrugged. 'I'm not a gourmet or anything, but I can get by. I find cooking relaxing, don't you?'

Oh, um… She swallowed. 'It just seems like another chore to me.'

He stilled and then he swung around, his eyes narrowing in on her face and at the way she worried at the water ring. One corner of his mouth lifted and her blood chugged. 'Can't cook, huh?'

Sprung. She refused to show any regret on that front, though. 'Can't say I've had much use for cooking.'

He placed a chopping board on the table and proceeded to dice an onion. 'What do you eat, then?'

His fingers were deft and while he was nowhere near as speedy as the celebrity chefs she sometimes watched on the television, he was quick enough and relaxed into the bargain.

'Tash?'

She suddenly realised she'd been staring at him slicing and dicing, completely caught up in the rhythm of it. She forced her gaze from his hands. She didn't want to think about his hands.

Of course, all she could then think about was Mitch's hands. Doing things they had no right doing and things she had no right thinking about.

Don't go there.

She cleared her throat. 'On the days I go into work I usually get a hot meal at the pub. The bistro does your average pub grub—schnitzel and salad, bangers and mash, calamari and chips.'

'What do you do for your other meals of the day?'

She shrugged. 'Cereal.'

He stopped chopping—tomatoes this time—to stare at her. 'You mean breakfast cereal?'

Her shoulders started to inch up towards her ears. She forced them back down. 'I like cereal. I get the healthy stuff.' Most of the time.

'You eat cereal for dinner?'

'Sometimes. So what? Can't you chop and talk at the same time?'

'Can you cook anything?'

'I can fry an egg.' Though she hardly ever did. 'Do beans on toast count?'

'I…' He shrugged. 'Sure, why not.' He sent her a quick glance. 'What about salad?'

'I buy that pre-packaged stuff from the supermarket. I don't see why you'd go to the trouble of chopping all that stuff up if you can buy it already made.'

'Because it's fresher and might taste better?'

'Or if you were counting your pennies,' she added as an afterthought. 'Luckily, these days I don't have to worry about that.'

She, Rick and Mitch had all grown up in a solidly working class neighbourhood. Money had been an issue for a lot of people.

Had it for Mitch and his parents? He'd been too far ahead of her in school for her to know much about him. It occurred to her then that he hadn't offered up much information about himself when he'd first befriended her either.

Her lips twisted. Unlike her. Had he played her or what?

You're in his cabin. He's keeping you safe. He just argued your case to his superiors. Cut the guy some slack. For heaven's sake, he's cooking you dinner!

Eight years ago he'd only been twenty-two. So young. She hadn't factored that in. Maybe because she'd slammed a lid on those memories and hadn't let them see the light of day since.

'You like your job at the Royal Oak?'

There was a hint of that *you shouldn't be working in a pub* disapproval that she so often got, a hint of disbelief that a barmaid might, in fact, enjoy her job.

'Yeah, I do.' She rested her elbows on the table as if his disapproval didn't bother her in the slightest. 'I'm good at what I do. I like our regulars and get on well with them. They treat me with respect.'

A smile played around the corners of his mouth. 'What?' she demanded. 'You're not going to tell me nice girls don't work in pubs, are you? Because I have news for you—I'm not a nice girl.'

He threw his head back and laughed. The sound filled the cabin with warmth. It filled her with warmth. She stared at him. She couldn't help it.

'I was going to say that I hear you run a tight ship. The regulars show you respect because they know if they step out of line they'll be out on their ear.'

She grinned down at her hands. 'Saves a lot of time in the long run.'

'I keep waiting to hear that you've bought the place.'

'The pub?' She gaped at him. 'Me?'

'Why not?'

'Oh, I don't know,' she drawled. 'But maybe the fact I don't have any business qualifications or accountancy skills might do for a start.'

'You could get them,' he challenged. 'Rumour has it that you've singlehandedly turned that hotel around.'

'Rumour exaggerates. I merely had some ideas that Clarke let me put into practice. I had support. The staff at the pub are great. We're a good team.' She frowned. 'Have you heard rumours that Clarke is selling?'

'No.'

She shook her head. She didn't want to own a pub. She was happy with things just the way they were. She pulled herself back into the here and now and nodded towards the chopping board. 'What are you making?'

'A big batch of savoury mince.' He stilled before setting his knife down. 'I didn't ask if there's anything you don't eat.'

'I'm not fussy.' She couldn't have afforded to be, growing up with her father.

'What's your favourite meal?'

'Fish and chips.' The days her father had brought fish and chips home for dinner had been good days—days she'd been able to relax her guard and breathe a bit easier. 'What about you?' she found herself asking. Given her reaction to him this morning, it seemed amazing to her that they could be talking like this.

'Beef Wellington.'

She knew what it was but she'd never tried it.

'The beauty of savoury mince is that we can use it to make shepherd's pie tonight, cottage pie tomorrow and have it with rice the night after.'

'If one has to cook then I can see the attraction in that,' she said. 'As long as you like savoury mince.' She had to choke back a laugh at the look he sent her. 'Relax. Savoury mince is fine by me.'

'It could get monotonous.'

She kept her face deadpan. 'Do you have cereal?'

'Yes.'

She knew he did. She'd checked earlier. 'Then I'll be fine.'

One side of his mouth hooked up. 'Glad that's sorted.'

She flashed back to the moment on the beach earlier when he'd been about to tell her why he'd joined the police force and her far from civil response. The memory of that other moment when she'd almost physically lashed out at him still made her stomach churn. She had to find a way to get through the next few days without doing something she'd regret forever…and without losing her marbles. She poured herself another glass of water. 'Uh, Mitch, I've been less than gracious today.'

He'd brought too many memories hurtling back.

'I want to apologise. We're never going to agree about Rick so I propose we postpone any further discussion about him until we leave here.'

He stilled from where he'd started browning mince in the frying pan. 'You mean that?'

'I can't see that it'll help us achieve anything.'

'And what do you want to achieve?'

'I'd like us to get through the next couple of days as peacefully as we can.' And with her self-respect intact. It wasn't just memories that Mitch had brought rushing back but those same feelings of desire and need too. Back then, she hadn't known how to deal with them but she was a grown woman now. Lashing out at every opportunity was not the mature thing to do. It was time to get a grip on herself.

'You won't get an argument from me on that head, Tash.'

She counted up the number of times he'd apologised to her today. It had to have been at least five. She swallowed. 'So you accept my apology?'

'Yes.

She let out a breath she hadn't known she'd been holding. 'Thank you.'

He didn't say anything else. He added ingredients to the mince and continued stirring. She moistened her lips again, her throat so dry she wasn't sure she could form coherent words. 'So—' she gulped more water '—why was it you decided to become a police officer?'

He didn't turn around again immediately. He measured out a glass of water and poured it over the mince, added some stuff in jars. Eventually he put the lid on the frying pan and lowered the heat. 'You know what, Tash? I think you were right earlier. I don't think it's any of your business after all.'

Her head rocked back. It took all of her strength to school the shock from her face, though nothing could alleviate the sting from her soul.

'That needs to simmer for half an hour. I'm going to take a quick shower.'

He took the backpack and left the cabin.

She drained the glass of water. 'Right,' she murmured to the silence.

With eyes that were too hot she rose and walked down to the beach, praying the evening cool would find a way to soothe the tempest raging inside her.

CHAPTER FOUR

MITCH CLOCKED THE exact moment Tash peeped around the blanket and into the main room of the cabin. He didn't need to check his watch. He'd done that five minutes ago—one forty-five a.m. The release of sleep obviously eluded her, as it did him. Given the scenario he'd presented her with this morning, it was hardly surprising.

The extent of her anger and resentment towards him throughout the day *had* surprised him, though, which was why her suggestion of a truce had blown him completely out of the water.

He sat up. Some inner voice warned him it'd be wiser to feign sleep, but he ignored it. 'Can't sleep?'

She moved more fully into the room. 'Sorry, I didn't mean to disturb you.'

'You didn't.' It hadn't been her restless tossing and turning in the next room, but an unfamiliar heat that prickled his skin and scorched his thoughts that had kept him awake. His lips twisted. And an all too familiar heat balled in his groin. He didn't know why Tash affected him like this. He knew prettier women. He sure as heck knew more welcoming women. It was useless denying it, though. Something in her called to something in him.

He blew out a breath. 'I can't sleep either.'

'Is the sofa uncomfortable?'

'Not at all.' It was a big old blousy thing that let him stretch out his full length. He couldn't blame the sofa.

He'd left a night lamp burning in the kitchen and in the faint glow it cast out he saw the way she bit her lip, the way one foot rubbed back and forth over the other. 'Are you worried you're not safe out here?'

She wore a pair of soft cotton shorts in an indeterminate grey that came down to her knees and a faded red T-shirt. Her hair was tousled—testament to her tossing and turning—and she didn't wear a scrap of make-up.

The burn in his groin intensified. He gritted his teeth and tried to ignore it. *Professionalism.*

Another glance at her—at those turned down

lips—and he wanted to pat the sofa beside him, wrap an arm around those slim shoulders and give her all the reassurance she needed.

Ha! If he tried that she'd deck him. He forced himself to focus on her needs rather than the insistent ache of his body. 'I'm confident danger won't follow us here. That said, I'll feel better when this is all over.' When he knew that she was safe.

She lifted a foot and rubbed it against the back of her calf. 'Me too.'

She had nicely toned calves. In fact, she had nice legs all round. Spectacular, in fact and—

Stop staring!

She smoothed her hair down. 'I know that sitting up all night thinking about it isn't going to prove particularly productive.'

'No.' Unfortunately, the only idea that came to him to take her mind off the situation was illicit, forbidden and would rightfully earn him a black eye and a knee to the groin. It'd have her tearing out of here and putting herself in the way of danger too. He fisted his hands in the blanket and dragged in a deep breath.

'What I need is a generous glass of red.' That

foot made another journey up her calf. 'That'd make me drowsy enough to sleep.'

It travelled back down to rest on the floor. He jerked back. Did he have any wine in the place? He didn't drink much wine.

'Mind you, it'd only give me nightmares in the end so it'd probably be a false economy anyway.'

He hauled himself off the sofa. She took a step back as if the movement had startled her and he made himself slow and gentle his strides. 'I might have just the thing.'

Brandy. He opened a kitchen cupboard and reached right to the back. Yep—as he'd hoped—a new bottle. It was a nice bottle too.

He poured them both generous snifters. Carrying the glasses in one hand and with the bottle tucked under his arm, he opened the cabin door and stepped outside. All the time he was careful not to move too close to her. He didn't want to spook her any more than she already was. In fact, he didn't even speak again, but after a brief hesitation she followed him.

He sat to one side of the front step and set the glasses down. She settled on the other side of the step a good arm's length away. The cool night air and the scent of the sea eased the tightness inside him.

She picked up one of the glasses and sniffed. 'I don't like Scotch.'

'It's brandy.'

She wrinkled her nose. 'They smell the same to me.'

'Heathen!' He feigned outrage, picking up his glass. 'What kind of barmaid are you?'

It was lighter out here in the moon and starlight than inside and he watched as one side of her mouth kinked upwards. She stuck her nose in the air. 'I'll have you know that I'm a hotel manager not a barmaid.'

'Same difference.'

A sound left her that was almost a laugh and more of that tightness eased out of him.

'Try it. Just a sip. You might be pleasantly surprised.' He swirled the brandy in his glass, brought it to his nose before taking a generous sip. He held the liquid in his mouth for a moment, savouring its warmth before swallowing and sharing the smoky heat with his throat and stomach.

She watched him. Closely. Just how closely

made his stomach clench. And then she copied his actions. Her nose wrinkled as if waiting for a bad taste, but after a moment her face cleared. 'Okay, that's not so bad. Maybe I could get used to this stuff after all.'

On the surface she was remarkably cool, but as he stared at her hands—at the way they cupped the glass—the tension wound up tight inside him again. 'Tash, I've never had a premeditated threat of violence directed at me.' The violence he'd experienced had been immediate—violence he'd been ready for, violence he'd been trained to counter and deal with.

She didn't say anything.

'I imagine it's pretty frightening.'

She stared down into her glass with a frown. 'There's a part of me that just can't seem to take it seriously.' She lifted an eyebrow—at the glass, not at him. 'I'm no stranger to anger and fighting. I've seen more pub brawls than I can count on both hands, and I've broken a lot of them up. Before that there was my father. With all of that, though, I knew where the threat was coming from, but this...' She lifted her head and met his gaze. 'It's alien to me.'

There was nothing to say to that. He just nodded and tried to swallow the bile that rose in his throat.

'That flash of temper which makes someone strike out—I understand that. I don't condone it, but I understand it. And I know how to read the signs. What I don't understand is cold-bloodedly plotting to hurt someone.'

'People do it.' He kept his voice even. He didn't want to frighten her, but he wanted her to remain on her guard.

'Yes.' The word was nothing but a sigh.

Talking about this threat, worrying about it and picking at it wouldn't help her relax. 'Tell me something.'

'What?'

'What made you offer a truce this afternoon?'

She stilled for a long moment and then seemed to mentally shake herself. 'Oh, that.' She turned from staring into her glass.

Yes, that. He wanted to trust her, but he didn't.

For a fraction of a second her nostrils flared. 'That flash of violence we just spoke about... I found myself in the grip of it earlier. I nearly hit you.'

His head rocked back and it felt as if a giant fist tightened about his chest squeezing until he could hardly breathe.

'I've never hit someone in temper before. I've not even come close to it.' She stared into the night and he sensed her revulsion simmering just below the surface. Revulsion aimed at herself this time, not him. 'I never want to be pushed to those limits again.'

He'd done a job on this woman, no doubt about it. He hadn't meant to, but that was no excuse. 'I had landed you with a corker this morning, Tash. That kind of shock can emerge in any number of confronting ways, including bursts of temper. Don't be too hard on yourself.'

'Perhaps.' She stared back down into her glass. 'But it wasn't just that. Being forced to spend time in your company along with the whole Rick déjà vu thing hurtled me back into the past and to how I felt back then. Today's events ripped the lid off all of that. The result was…well, you saw.'

Bile burned his throat. He couldn't take a sip of brandy now if his life depended on it.

'I know you apologised, and I believe you meant it, but…'

She didn't go on. He didn't know whether to be sorry or relieved. 'You shouldn't have bottled that stuff up. Why didn't you talk to someone?'

She gave a laugh devoid of mirth and raised a snarky eyebrow. 'Who? Who could I have talked to, Mitch? My father?'

He closed his eyes.

'You'd taken my best friend away.'

Rick. He cracked his eyes back open. 'You must've had girlfriends.'

'All who blamed me for Rick's arrest.'

For a moment he thought he might throw up.

'Just as I'd have blamed them if the situation had been reversed. Because the sad fact of the matter is if I hadn't taken you to the party that night you'd never have discovered the drugs. Therefore, Rick would never have been arrested.'

'Not then, maybe.'

She merely shrugged.

He tried to swallow but couldn't. The world Tash had grown up in had been harsh and inflexible, the people unyielding to outsiders and unforgiving of their own. Mitch had effectively ostracised her from her community.

You put a drug supplier behind bars. Rick had

possessed a lot of influence over Tash. By arresting Rick he might, in fact, have saved her from a drug overdose. He might have saved her life.

'Besides, trusting you hadn't turned out all that well for me so it wasn't an exercise I was eager to repeat.'

Do you know I never trusted another man after what you did? Her earlier words haunted him.

'Given all that, why aren't you still actively hating me?'

'Maybe I do.' She squinted out into the darkness. 'Or maybe it's finally run its course.' She lifted her head. 'Yes, that's what it feels like— as if today was some kind of catharsis. I no longer hate you for the same reason I no longer hate my father.'

She put him in the same category as her father? A wave of tiredness so black swept over him, blotting out the light from the moon and the stars.

'I don't know if you remember what it's like to be a kid, Mitch.' He stiffened. His arms broke out in goose flesh. 'But it's something I can never forget. One has so little power as a minor. You're always at the mercy of other people's whims and impulses.'

He remembered. Bile burned his throat. Oh, yes, how well he remembered.

She turned to him. 'But I'm no longer a child. I'm the one who calls the shots in my life now. My father can no longer hurt me. Neither can you.'

Her words opened up an abyss inside him. 'Tash,' he croaked. 'I—'

'I'm not saying this to make you feel guilty. You were only twenty-two. I forgot how young you were.'

'If I could go back and change how I dealt with it all, I would.'

'So you say.' There was a surprising lack of bitterness in her voice. 'But that's no longer here nor there to me. If you need to square something with your conscience then that's your affair. What I think shouldn't matter.'

It did if he wanted her friendship.

He reared back. What was he thinking? She would *never* trust him again.

'You didn't move to the Western suburbs of Sydney until you were twelve, right?'

She had a good memory.

'And your family was what—middle class… white-collar?'

'I lived with my grandparents. My grandfather was an accountant.' He was careful to keep all inflection from his voice.

'So money was never an issue?'

'No, I was lucky.' He forced those words out. 'I had opportunities.' Opportunities kids like Tash and Rick had never had.

She nodded. 'You were never one of us and that helps too. You didn't really know what you were doing.'

He'd been getting a criminal off the street!

But he knew that wasn't what she meant, and he didn't want to start fighting with her again so he kept his mouth shut.

'You see, if you'd been through what me and Rick and Cheryl and the rest of us had experienced I do think you might've acted differently.'

He stilled.

'It doesn't change what happened, but it means I can look on you with a kinder eye than I might otherwise.'

He stared out into the night and raked a hand through his hair.

'You asked,' she finally said.

And she'd given him one heck of an answer.

And he didn't want to talk about this anymore. 'Where were you going to go for your holiday?'

She didn't even blink at the change in subject. 'North. I'd have liked to have made it as far as Byron Bay. I've never been there, but I've heard lots about it. It's supposed to be very beautiful, but it's a long way—at least a ten-hour drive. I was going to drive as far as Coffs Harbour today and then see how I felt. Five nights in Coffs sounded awfully nice too.'

Coffs Harbour was probably the midway point between Sydney and Byron Bay. It was a nice-sized town with plenty to do.

'What did you have planned for those five nights?'

'Besides swimming, reading a novel or two and eating takeaway every night?'

'Besides that.' He could provide her with the beach for swimming. He had a bookcase full of books. They couldn't do takeaway but he could cook a burger on the barbecue. He could also do a mean steak and salad. The cabin might be rustic but he always ate well when he was here. He mentally stowed the leftover savoury mince in the freezer.

She rested her arms on her knees, her brandy clasped lightly in her fingers. The moon wove silver streaks through her hair and eyelashes until she looked almost ethereal. An ache started up deep inside him. He'd hurt this woman badly. He'd like to make it up to her if he could. He'd do everything to keep her safe, and if he could help her forget for a few hours here and there about Rick and the violence he had planned for her, then he'd do that too.

He topped up her brandy, careful not to get too close. 'Well?' he prompted.

'I wanted to try my hand at something I hadn't done before, like surfboarding or something. I thought I could get some lessons. And maybe I'd have ridden around on one of those paddleboats for a bit.'

'Sounds like fun.'

Her lips twisted in a rueful smile. 'Yeah, it does. And I haven't had any real time off in over three years.'

'Three years!' He gaped at her. She'd been in

permanent full-time employment all of that time. 'That's illegal!'

She snorted. 'What? Going to arrest me?'

'Someone needs to have a word with Clarke,' he growled. Tash deserved something better than working in a pub, being a *slave* in a pub.

'Staff turnover, Clarke's mother got sick et cetera et cetera. Time got away. None of it was planned. Clarke and I came to a financial arrangement that suited us both.'

She'd wanted to build a nest egg, to have a financial security blanket. He understood that, but—

'So butt out.'

He raised his hands. 'Butting out.' They both sipped their brandy.

'So what else were you going to do on this holiday of yours?'

'I wanted to do something different, out of the ordinary like…'

He leaned towards her, intrigued at the way she broke off. 'Like?'

'You'll think it's dumb…'

Now she really had his attention. 'Try me.'

She lifted one shoulder and rubbed her chin

against it before reaching up to scratch her shoulder. 'There's a native wildlife sanctuary just outside of Coffs. They rescue injured wildlife plus they have a koala-breeding programme. There's all sorts of wildlife there—echidnas, possums and emus. You can even feed the kangaroos.' She shook out her hair, not looking at him. 'I was going to spend a day there, take a picnic and make a donation. I thought it sounded...fun.'

A smile lit his insides. 'Beneath that smart-mouth tough-cookie exterior you're nothing but a big softie.'

The eyes she turned to him, though, had seen too much hard experience and he sobered.

He pulled a breath into cramped lungs and tried not to focus on the tempting allure of her lips. 'I don't think that's dumb. I think it sounds kind of nice. It sounds like a good place to support.' He'd bet her father had never taken her to the zoo. At least his father—

He cut the thought off.

She looked at him then. Really looked at him and it made his gut clench. Her gaze lowered to his lips and more than just his stomach tightened. He swore he could see the flare of gold in her eyes, but it was abruptly cut off. She moved away from him, even though there was a significant distance between them already.

Was she worried he'd try and close that gap?

In one fluid motion she rose to her feet. 'I believe the brandy did the trick. Thanks, Mitch.'

He could've sworn, though, that she'd have preferred to call him Officer King. He called a goodnight after her. He did what he could to make his mind blank, but Tash filled it.

She hadn't had a holiday in three years? He gave a low whistle. Bradford couldn't have timed his vendetta at a worse time if he'd tried. He…

Mitch stiffened. A grim black seam of something hard and unyielding solidified inside him. If Bradford had been in contact with Tash, maybe he'd timed it exactly as he'd wanted to? Maybe he'd meant to attack at the precise moment Tash would least likely be missed?

In the dark his hand clenched. She wasn't a stupid woman. She couldn't know the kind of man Rick had become.

He meant to make sure she didn't find out first-hand. In the meanwhile, sitting around and brooding on it would send her stir-crazy. He had to come up with something, and fast.

Tash glanced up from washing her breakfast bowl to find Mitch staring at her. His regard made her pulse leap. 'What?' She grabbed a tea towel and started wiping vigorously.

'I had a thought last night.'

Her hands stilled. 'About how to bring this situation to a quick conclusion?'

He shifted his weight. 'That's out of my jurisdiction, I'm afraid.'

If it had been left up to him would he have let her ring Rick? She shook the thought off. What did it matter now anyhow? He continued to survey her and the expression on his face kept shifting so she couldn't get a proper handle on him. One moment he looked as if he expected her to yell at him—the kicked-puppy expression. The next he looked as if he'd like to gobble her up—starting at her toes and slowly moving upwards until he'd explored every inch of her. Her toes curled. 'A thought?' she choked out.

He nodded at the bowl she still rubbed. 'Are you done there?'

'Uh, sure.'

She set it on the shelf. In the next moment she found her hand enclosed in his as he hauled her out of the door. 'Ta-da!' He dropped her hand with a flourish and gestured to a kayak.

Her jaw fell open. She glanced at him out of the corner of her eyes. 'Okay.' She drew the word out.

He rolled his shoulders. 'Look, I know it's not a surfboard or a paddleboat, but I thought this might be fun.'

She swung to him as their conversation from the previous evening came back to her. *I wanted to try my hand at something I hadn't done before.* She'd never kayaked before. She walked around it. 'Where did you manage to dig this up from?'

'I've had it leaning against the back of the cabin beneath some canvas.'

That'd explain all of the banging and thumping earlier.

'And I've made sure it's completely spider-free.'

She appreciated that.

'So…' He rubbed the back of his neck and glanced at her from disconcertingly blue eyes. 'What do you think?'

For some reason his uncertainty touched her. And she had to give him credit—he really was trying to make this ordeal as easy for her as he could. She glanced at the kayak and then at the blue glitter of the beach below. Excitement shifted through her. 'You're going to teach me how to drive this thing?'

'That's the plan.'

'And we're allowed to go outside this little bay here to explore?'

'Yep.'

'Then I think it sounds perfect!'

He grinned. It made her blink. She made herself look back at the kayak. *He's an attractive man, but you can't go there again.*

Ha! Tell that to her pulse!

She pulled in a breath. She was tired. This was a strange situation. Everything was bound to feel topsy-turvy.

'Okay, how's this for a plan? We make up a picnic—we can stow it here in the front.' He slapped a hand down on the...bow? Was that what it was called? 'And then we head up along the coast until we feel we've had enough, stop to eat and then head back?'

That sounded great, but… 'Are you allowed to do that?'

He shrugged. 'Sure.'

He didn't say anything more and she didn't press him for details. She lifted a paddle. 'I'm used to carrying trays of drinks and hefting the odd keg into place, but I don't know how long I could paddle for.'

'That won't matter. If you get tired you can take it easy. I'm used to it.'

She eyed him uncertainly. 'You sure you won't mind picking up my slack?'

'Tash, this is supposed to be an exercise in fun and frivolity—a bit of R & R—not something to stress about.'

'Oh, okay.' She nibbled her lip. 'I'm a bit out of practice with that.' And she wasn't used to not pulling her own weight. She shook herself. 'Something I can do, however, is make sandwiches.'

He whistled in mock admiration and she was tempted to give him a playful push…but that would mean touching him. It'd mean pressing her hand against that tanned firm flesh and—

Stop it!

'So how about I pack a picnic?' Her voice came out at a squeak. 'While you do whatever needs doing with the kayak?'

'Sounds good to me.'

She raced back inside. She stood in the kitchen for several long moments before remembering what she was about and kicking herself into action.

When Tash had finished making sandwiches and had put them into an airtight plastic container, Mitch stowed them into a waterproof sack with bottles of water. She handed him a couple of apples. He raised an eyebrow. 'That's not holiday food.'

She shrugged. 'They fill you up when you're hungry, though.'

He added them to the sack and then reached for a packet of shortbread cream biscuits and waggled them at her before adding them to the bounty too. 'That's holiday food. C'mon.'

He hoisted the sack onto his shoulder and she followed him down to the beach, where he'd already taken the kayak. He shot her a grin. 'Excited?'

Right on cue, her stomach started to flutter and

she found herself smiling back. She shrugged, though, struggling for casual. It wouldn't do to jump up and down like a little kid. 'Sure.'

She had a feeling, though, that he saw through her pretence of unconcern.

She shrugged the thought off. She had a feeling she wasn't as perturbed by that as she should be, but she was determined to enjoy the sun and sea and the novelty of learning something new.

'Right, you sit in the front.'

He held the kayak steady while she settled herself where he indicated. He pushed them off and slid in behind her in one smooth motion. It made her mouth dry when she realised how fit he must be to do that all so effortlessly.

She shook herself and settled her cap on her head more securely. It was early—neither of them had slept late—and the air was still cool. She relished the feel of it against the bare skin of her arms…and the contrast to all of the latent strength and heat at her back. She swallowed and tried to dismiss that thought. 'I, uh…the motion is so smooth.'

'We're lucky. It's very calm today.'

There was something in his voice… No, there

was something no longer in his voice—a tension, a strain—and its absence made him sound younger, freer. She wanted to turn to look.

And then she was glad she couldn't.

Mitch gave her a few instructions and soon they were working in sync without needing to exchange a word. They turned right out of Mitch's tiny bay and headed north along the coast. They were only about a hundred metres offshore, but the swell was gentle and the four solid weeks of recent fine weather ensured the water was clear. She gave herself up to the buoyancy of the kayak and the freshness of the morning.

'Look.' Mitch tapped her shoulder and pointed downwards. Below them swam a large stingray, flapping along as easily and lightly as they did.

A sigh eased out of her. 'Beautiful,' she breathed, drawing the scent of the ocean into her lungs. 'It's so quiet out here.'

The only sounds were the soft splashing of their paddles, the lapping of water against the kayak and the sound of birdsong onshore.

'It's why I prefer a kayak to a speedboat. I'm sure waterskiing and all of that speed is fun, but...'

She could almost feel the way he lifted a shoulder in a shrug. 'But nothing could beat the tranquillity of this,' she finished for him.

'The quiet doesn't scare you?'

Not when he had her back. She shook her head.

'No?'

She realised he'd misinterpreted the action. 'I...' She moistened her lips. 'I can see why the quiet and solitude might intimidate some people, but...' She remembered the bliss of the silence when she and Rick had taken off camping as teenagers. 'But I like it. The city is never quiet. This is...'

She stiffened.

'What?' he demanded.

'Relaxing,' she finally said. 'This is relaxing.' Surely she'd relaxed at some stage during the last three or four years? One didn't need a holiday to relax.

She bit her lip. Sure she had.

But not like this.

CHAPTER FIVE

TASH SHRUGGED THE unsettling thought aside—something she'd been doing a lot since being landed with Mitch's company. She'd revisit it later. Who knew? It might be a good thing, all of this revisiting issues from the past. Maybe she could lay them to rest and…

And what?

She waved a hand in front of her face. 'How far along the coastline have you explored?'

'I've been miles and miles in both directions. Sometimes I pack a picnic and make a day of it—stop somewhere for a swim and lunch. Sometimes I only take the kayak out for an hour.'

A sigh whispered out of her. If she stayed here longer maybe she'd get a chance to—

She blinked. What on earth…? That was a crazy thought and one definitely not worth revisiting! She couldn't wait to get home and for things to return to normal.

They manoeuvred around a rocky outcrop. A flash of movement caught her eye. She leaned forward so quickly the kayak rocked. 'A seal!'

Behind her, Mitch chuckled and did something to steady them. 'He suns himself there pretty regularly.'

A seal! She'd seen a seal! She sat dazed for a moment before remembering to paddle again.

They continued at a leisurely pace until Tash lost all sense of time. She saw seagulls diving for fish, pelicans gliding along the surface of the water, another stingray and a school of silver fish. The peace of the day and the warmth of the sun and the feeling of being at one with nature filtered into her soul until she felt light and warm and right.

Mitch touched her shoulder and his finger seemed to linger there a couple of beats too long. A pulse started beating in her throat. 'Can you see that there?' He pointed.

She blinked and did her best to follow the direction of his finger rather than on the warmth that lingered at her shoulder. She shaded her eyes and ordered them to focus. 'Um...' She cleared her throat. 'What is it?'

'A sea cave.'

She almost swung to look at him, more sure of herself now in the kayak, but then she remembered the heat in his eyes last night that had rivalled the burn of the brandy in her stomach, and she resisted the urge. 'A sea cave? Have you ever been in there?'

'Uh huh.' He moved them towards it. 'You want to see?'

She stared at the opening that emerged in the rock…at the darkness beyond. 'I, uh…take it it's safe?'

'It is at low tide, which it is now.'

It was? She glanced around, feeling like an ignorant landlubber.

'Are you claustrophobic?'

She shook her head.

'Shall I take us inside?'

A shiver—part fear, part anticipation as if she were about to embark on a roller coaster ride—shook her. 'Yes, please.' This sea cave reminded her of the Aladdin's Cave picture books she'd borrowed from the school library once.

She rested her paddle across her knees and Mitch swung the kayak into the narrow opening. The tunnel lasted for maybe five or six metres before opening out into a shallow pool with a tiny shell-encrusted beach at its far end. Fissures in the rock above let in long shafts of light. Salt crystals lining the interior sparkled silver all around them, turning the cave into a glittering fairyland.

Her mouth formed a perfect O. 'I've never seen anything like this in my life,' she whispered. 'This is like something from *Arabian Nights*.' On impulse she turned to him. He did something with his paddle so the kayak barely moved in response to her movement. 'May I take a shell as a souvenir?'

The half-light softened his face, turning him into a sort of soft focus angel. The longer she stared at him the more he came into focus. And then he smiled. She blinked and forced her eyes back to the front. Her heart pounded. 'I, um…' Darn it! Work, brain! Work, mouth! 'That is if you don't mind.'

Her voice croaked out of her, but he didn't say anything, just moved them towards the tiny beach and she wondered if he'd noticed her reaction— her momentary fascination with him.

Fascination, huh? Is that what you call it?

She clenched her eyes shut.

Her breathing grew more erratic rather than less. She tried telling herself it was the exertion of paddling, but it wasn't. Mitch had a smile that could make a woman forget which way was up. A flicker of heat licked low in her belly. She swallowed and clenched her thighs together. Mitch had a kind of face that could make a woman forget vows she'd made to herself—vows to never fall for him again, to not expose herself to his treachery.

Only he wasn't being treacherous at the moment, was he? He was trying to give her a holiday.

He wants Rick behind bars. Again.

But that didn't really have anything to do with her. He hadn't asked her anything about Rick so far today, hadn't tried to find out if she knew Rick's whereabouts or how the police could find him.

They landed against the beach with a tiny bump and scrape. Mitch vaulted lightly out and she barely noticed the gentle rock from side to side he steadied it again so quickly. He reached out to take her hand. 'Keep your shoes on. The shells are sharp.'

She put her hand in his, all of his latent power pressed against her palm, and curled around her fingers in undiscovered promise as he pulled her upright and helped her step out of the kayak. Her heart fluttered up into her throat, nearly smothering her. 'Thank you.' Her voice came out breathy, thready.

He let go of her and she had to lock her knees to stay upright. She glanced around, forced herself to feign interest in her surroundings rather than the man beside her. At the very back of the cave where it was darkest a couple of straggly plants clung to the rock—obviously a place where the tide rarely reached. 'It'd be possible to hide away from the world in here.'

She had a sudden vision of a thick blanket spread on the smoother ground beyond the shells, a bottle of champagne, strawberries…and a naked man.

The vision of her and Mitch making love here hit her hard and hot. Heat pooled between her legs, her breasts grew heavy and her lips parted. She shot a look at him from beneath heavy eyelids—took in his wide shoulders, the depth of his chest and those rippling biceps.

He'd be sheer heaven to touch.

She lifted her gaze to find him staring down at her. Her tongue inched out to touch her lips, moisten them…sensitize them.

He backed up, his face suddenly tight. 'Pick your shell, Tash.'

The warning in his voice slapped her like a dash of icy water. She snapped away and crouched down, scrabbling wildly. This…this desire was just a carry-over from eight years ago when she'd been a crazy stupid teenager.

Except…

She'd never wanted him with this kind of carnal heat back then.

And there were more reasons than she could count why she should resist the pull now.

Her hand closed about a shell—a fan, grey on the outside and pink on the inside. She rose to her feet. 'Thank you.'

Thank you for the adventure.

Thank you for the reminder.

Without another word they climbed back into the kayak and paddled away.

* * *

They emerged back into the sunlight and Mitch had to fight the urge to swear. His head pounded, his groin pounded and his knuckles had turned a sickly white around the paddle. With a superhuman effort he pulled air into his lungs and loosened his grip.

He ached with every atom of his being to turn the boat towards the shore and make for it with all the speed his body possessed, to spread the towels on the beach and lay Tash down on them and—

Real professional!

'I think it might be time to head home.'

His words emerged wooden, forbidding and non-negotiable. Not what he'd intended. Tash's back stiffened and he grimaced and silently cursed. Why couldn't he find a speck of moderation around this woman?

She tossed her head. 'I feel as if I could keep kayaking all day.'

Her attempt to drag this tension-filled, gut-wrenching moment back within the realms of normality didn't stop him from wanting her either.

Yesterday she might've acted like a brat but today she was all woman. In more ways than one. His knuckles turned white again. 'Believe me, your back and shoulders will be sore enough tomorrow as it is.'

An hour later, when they turned back into the cove leading up to the cabin, he'd formulated a plan. First, though, he had to get them safely back onto the beach.

The surf had started to build so he brought the kayak in on an angle, straightening when they caught a wave that they rode all the way into shore without incident. Tash let out a cry of delight that she cut off too quickly. The grin that had built inside him at the exhilaration slid off his face.

He pulled the kayak up onto the beach. Tash scrambled out without waiting for him to offer his hand. He seized her towel and spread it out on the sand. He set the cooler bag with their lunch beside it. 'You wanted some sun and surf.' He bowed, doing his utmost to keep this low-key. 'It all awaits.'

She bit her lip and glanced at the kayak. 'You don't need any help with...anything?'

'Nope.'

He wanted her down here, enjoying herself and in holiday mode. He needed to get up to the cabin and away from her as fast as he could. He needed a chance to get his head screwed on straight again. He needed to remember why they were here.

She pulled her sunglasses from her shorts pocket and settled them high on her nose and pulled the brim of her cap down low. She sat on her towel without another word.

He hovered uncertainly. Eventually she deigned to glance at him. 'No doubt you have phone calls to make.' And just like that she extinguished the holiday mood. Her cool politeness, however, didn't dampen the fire that still raged within him.

He seized the sack with the phones and settled it on one shoulder. He lifted the kayak onto his other shoulder and set off for the cabin.

The minute he was inside he poured himself a glass of iced water and chugged it down. He collapsed to the sofa, head in hands. 'Damn it!' His job was to protect her, to keep her safe. She was vulnerable right now and seducing her would be unforgivable.

There mightn't be much seduction involved.

The expression on her face in the cave burned itself afresh on his brain and he groaned. He could not take advantage of her vulnerability. It'd be…

Divine? Amazing? The best?

It'd be despicable.

He rose and gulped down more iced water. He *wasn't* going to sleep with his reluctant house guest, and he *would* make her time here as pleasant as he could. It wouldn't erase the past, it wouldn't change the fact he'd hurt her, but it might mitigate it a little.

His lips twisted. Who on earth was he trying to help feel better—Tash or himself?

Perhaps both of them.

He shoved that thought aside and sat at the table. He needed to come up with a practical plan to get them through the rest of today and tomorrow and, if he needed to, the day after that. Detective Glastonbury would inform him as soon as Bradford was taken into custody, but until then they remained here. Stranded alone together.

He dragged a hand down his face. *Take it a day at a time.* All he had to figure out at the moment was how to get them through the rest of this afternoon and this evening *safely*. He thought hard. Eventually the tension in his shoulders eased and his breathing grew more regular. He could do this. *He could.*

Mitch glanced up from his spot on the sofa where he flicked through a computer magazine when Tash emerged from the bedroom. She'd come up from the beach mid-afternoon, had a shower and had then holed up in the bedroom for… He glanced at his watch. It was five o'clock. That made it two hours.

'I had a nap. Went out like a light.'

He wished she'd smile.

He closed the magazine. 'Holidays are hard work.' Her lips twisted but it was less of a smile than a grimace. He rushed on before she could remind him this was no holiday. 'You didn't get much sleep last night and it's amazing how much all of that swimming and kayaking can take out of you.'

'It was good tired,' she admitted. 'But now I need a coffee. Want one?'

'No, thanks.'

She made instant. He rolled his eyes. 'There's a coffee machine there, Tash.'

She shrugged. 'Takes too long. Too much fuss. I'm happy with instant.'

'Some things are worth taking their time over.'

His voice slid out like silk—smooth and suggestive. Her eyes flew to his, her cup halted halfway to her mouth. His gut tightened. *Crap!* He cleared his throat and battled to make his voice crisp, to banish any suggestiveness from it completely.

'You said you wanted to do new things on your holiday, right? To learn new things?' He couldn't let his guard down for a moment. As it was it took a Herculean effort to battle the urge to tease her further.

Her eyes narrowed. She finally took a sip of her coffee. 'Uh huh.'

'This afternoon I'm going to teach you to cook.'

She stared at him and lowered her mug. 'Mitch, I wanted to learn *fun* new things.'

'I'm going to teach you how to make a cake.'

She pursed her lips. She set her mug on the table and reached up behind to scratch between her shoulder blades. 'What kind?' she finally asked.

He let out a breath. 'Chocolate.'

'Won't it take me longer than an afternoon to learn how to do that?'

A rush of tenderness swept through him at her wide eyes. 'You'll be amazed how easy it is.'

'If that's the case, then…then can we make frosting too?'

'Chocolate butter frosting okay with you?'

Finally a smile touched her lips and he wanted to high-five someone. 'I'm not convinced the making will be fun, but the eating will be.' She rolled her eyes. 'Not that my hips need it.'

She slapped a hand to her rump. He followed the action. He went to say there was absolutely nothing wrong with her figure, that it was, in fact, spectacular, but she froze as if realising she'd just invited his view on the matter. They both looked away at the same time.

'Have a seat and finish your coffee,' he murmured, stumbling to his feet. 'I'll get the equipment and ingredients ready.'

He taught Tash how to make a cake. He barked

out instructions and she followed them to the letter—measuring, mixing and beating.

Correction—he tried to bark his instructions. He tried to keep his voice level and impersonal. But he found it almost impossible to keep the warmth out of his voice.

They laughed. Not a lot, but they laughed all the same and he couldn't remember the last time he'd felt so good.

As long as he remembered to keep his thoughts focused on the task at hand instead of the way her hair fell over her shoulders or how deft and clever her fingers were. Those fingers evoked images of—

He snapped to. 'I said beat the mixture. Put some back into it.'

She did as he said. She stopped a minute later, breathing hard. Would she breathe like that when she was making vigorous uninhibited love?

'This is harder work than paddling.'

He laughed. 'Baking as a workout? I hadn't thought of that before.'

'You could make a DVD combining an exercise workout with cooking. You could use your police credentials—Master Police Chef.'

'Cooking Bootcamp.'

And then they were both laughing.

She was a different woman from yesterday. Yesterday she'd radiated anger and resentment and badass attitude. But this afternoon... He swallowed. She wasn't just attractive—on every level—she was the most attractive woman he'd ever met.

Ever. His mouth dried.

Everything inside him gravitated towards her. It thrilled him to make her laugh, to bring a sparkle to her eyes. He thirsted to learn everything about her. And every atom of his body fired with a longing to make love with her. His heart hammered against his ribs. So much for professionalism.

He pulled in a breath. It'd only be unprofessional if he acted on it. He had to keep his head. Yesterday she'd hated him. He was jaded enough to know that today's turnaround might not be motivated by maturity but a need to get back at him, to revenge herself on him. She could be setting him up just to reject him. Payback.

He didn't want to believe it. It didn't square

with what he'd known about her eight years ago. Eight years was a long time, though, and people changed. And he truly didn't want to travel that path with her.

He regretted hurting her with every fibre that made him who he was, but her hurting him in return wouldn't do either of them any credit. And whether she knew it or not, it wouldn't make her feel better.

'How long do we cook it for?'

He snapped to and found she'd poured the mixture into the prepared cake tin. *Keep your head.* 'Forty minutes.'

She put the tin in the oven and then glanced at her watch and counted off forty minutes. 'How come you know how to make a cake from scratch without needing to follow a recipe?'

'My grandmother liked to bake.' It had brought her a measure of comfort on the bad days. And on those bad days he'd liked to keep her company so he'd feigned an interest. It had taken their minds off other things.

'What about your mum? Does she like to bake or is she like me?'

His gut screwed up, but he feigned outrage.

'What do you mean—like you? Are you telling me you didn't enjoy that?'

She stared back. Her hands went to her hips and he waited for her to challenge him, to delve further into areas where he didn't want to go. He clocked the moment she decided to bite her questions back. Whether she was after payback or not, he could see she was fighting to maintain her own distance.

Smart girl. But it made his heart sink all the same.

'I think the most pressing question, Tash, is how come you never learned to cook?'

She collected up the bowls and measuring jugs and other assorted paraphernalia they'd used and took them to the sink. 'There's no mystery there. My mother left when I was eight. My father didn't cook. So I had no one to teach me.' She said it without self-pity. 'I learned to heat up tinned food and make toast. That seemed sufficient at the time.'

He wanted to curse on her behalf. Instead he took her by the shoulders and led her from the sink and to a chair at the table. 'You made the cake so I clean up.'

She looked as if she might argue. In the end she just shrugged. 'Should I make the frosting now?'

'We don't want it to set yet, so no. We can't ice the cake,' he explained, 'until it's cooled or the icing melts and runs everywhere.'

'Oh, okay. That makes sense.'

'Have you ever seen her again? Your mother,' he clarified. 'Have you ever tried to find her?'

'Nope. She left me with a man who was too ready with his fists. I don't blame her for leaving, but I do blame her for leaving me in that situation. I'm not interested in knowing a person like that.'

Her words chilled him.

'Do you see your father any more?'

'Nope.'

She didn't expand. Questions chafed at him. Questions he had no right to ask—especially if he had no intention of answering her questions in return. Damn it! Why hadn't he dug deeper eight years ago and found out what had been really happening?

When he glanced at her there was a glint of laughter in her eyes. 'I'll tell you about me and my father if you tell me what happened to your parents. Did they abandon you with your grand-parents?'

Bile filled his mouth. 'They died when I was ten.'

Her head reared back. Her lips parted as her eyes widened. 'Oh, Mitch, that was truly clumsy of me. I'm sorry.'

He nodded.

'I mean I'm sorry I asked the way I did…and I'm sorry for your loss too, of course.'

Her face radiated sincerity. He nodded again. 'Thank you.'

Silence stretched between them. Eventually Tash cleared her throat. 'I, um…stood up to my father.'

He turned from the sink. 'You what?'

'I was eighteen and he came at me and I…um…decked him.'

He stared at her. Her father had been a big man.

'I didn't do it in anger. In fact I was quite clinical about it. I just wanted to stop him.'

This slip of a girl had stopped that six feet two inches and two hundred pounds worth of hard muscle?

'I've been doing judo since I was fifteen.'

'You have?'

'Rick talked me into it.'

He swallowed. In a lot of ways Rick had been a better friend to her than he'd ever been.

'It helped me to avoid the worst of my father's violence, to dodge it, but I'd always been too afraid to retaliate. One day, though, I was just tired of being frightened all the time.'

'Jeez, Tash!'

'I didn't break his ribs. I didn't break his nose or his arm.'

Had all those things happened to her?

'But I did set him on his backside and disabled him completely. And then I told him I would break each and every one of those things if he ever tried hitting me again.'

'What happened?'

'I moved out and we haven't spoken since.'

He saw it then. She refused to allow herself to ever be vulnerable to the people who'd hurt her, and who could blame her? They were supposed to have looked after her and taken care of her. Instead they'd betrayed her.

Just as he'd done.

* * *

Tash jumped when Mitch clapped his hands. 'Enough of that! This is a holiday, remember?'

That was an out-and-out lie, but she appreciated his efforts all the same.

'C'mon.'

He gestured for her to get up and she had to stifle a groan. 'Mitch, there was relaxation down on my list too, you know.'

'Oh, ye of little faith.'

He led her outside and she came up short when she saw a camp table and chair set up on the grass. The chair faced seaward. With his hands on her shoulders, he propelled her into that chair. 'Don't move.'

He disappeared, only to return a couple of minutes later. He set a glass of beer on the table in front of her, a bowl of mixed nuts and her fat novel. 'Happy hour.'

She stared at it all, her mouth agape.

'Relax, Tash. Enjoy my special homebrew, enjoy the view and relish just being.'

'What about you?' The minute the words left her mouth she could've bitten her tongue out. He'd made it plain that their relationship was strictly business, even if she did catch him looking at her with so much heat in his eyes at times she was afraid she'd spontaneously combust. She shifted on the chair. 'I mean I'm sure you've earned a chance to take the weight off too.'

'I'm all good.'

Now that was an understatement. *Stop it!* She seized the glass and took a gulp.

'What do you think?'

She took another sip. 'I'm not usually a fan of homebrew, but this isn't half bad.'

He laughed down at her. 'High praise indeed.'

'I'm a hotel manager.' She lifted her nose into the air. 'I know my beer.'

His grin lifted the right side of his mouth higher than his left. She couldn't look away. 'Enjoy it all while I go take care of dinner.'

She blinked. 'Thank you.' But she doubted he'd heard. By the time she'd managed to untangle her tongue he'd already vaulted onto the cabin's tiny veranda and was practically through the door.

Nobody had ever pampered her like this. Nobody had ever taken such pains to ensure she enjoyed herself. She stared at the view, but more often than not her eyes drifted back to the cabin.

Why was he being so nice to her? Especially when she'd been so awful to him yesterday?

Because he's a nice man.

She forced her gaze to the front and that glorious ocean view. She sipped the homebrew. She crunched a couple of nuts. He regretted hurting her eight years ago. She didn't want to acknowledge it—her resentment had provided her with a convenient shield—but it was the truth. She no longer doubted it. She scowled and selected a brazil nut, crunched it with extra ferocity. It didn't mean she had to forgive him, though.

She traced the pattern on the cover of her novel, glared at it. Okay, she could forgive him, but she didn't have to trust him. Yesterday where there'd been a roar and burn of resentment, today there was only a whisper and an ache.

She rolled her shoulders. She didn't hate Mitch any more. It was good to know.

She took another sip and then very carefully set her glass down. None of that changed the fact that Mitch believed Rick guilty of terrible crimes or that he would use her to bring about an arrest if he could.

Yeah, well, he could do it without her help. She

wasn't risking her heart like that a second time. Nor was she risking Rick's freedom again. She knew what Rick had done and what he hadn't done. Even if she wasn't at liberty to talk about it. A promise was a promise.

All the beauty in the view and the surroundings lost their appeal. If only…

'*Bon appétit!*'

Mitch appeared with a flourish. 'I'm sorry I can't manage takeaway pizza out here, but I thought homemade hamburgers might make a reasonable substitute. After all, they're nearly takeaway.'

For a crazy moment she had to fight back tears.

'Tash?'

She didn't know what to say. Surely she could trust him with the truth. They could keep it all unofficial and off the record, couldn't they?

'You don't like hamburgers?'

'I love hamburgers.' Her voice came out strangled.

He crouched down beside her. 'I swear I'm going to keep you safe. You don't need to worry.'

She shook her head. She couldn't tell him anything. Mitch and his job couldn't be separated.

Besides, he meant *his* idea of safe. But who was going to keep her heart safe from him?

'I know you will, Mitch.' She fought for a smile. 'This looks great.' Without another word she pulled her hamburger towards her and started to eat.

CHAPTER SIX

THE NEXT DAY Mitch took Tash fishing—another new experience. They sat on the rocks at one end of the bay and dangled fishing rods into the water for two hours.

The air barely moved and the sun warmed her skin with a customary benevolence she'd started to relish. Occasionally a swell of water would hit the rocks beneath them in a way that would lift it and send a fine spray of droplets over them. She could almost feel herself breathing in time to the swell of the sea, dragging in the mingled scents of salt, sea and eucalyptus into her lungs.

She and Mitch barely spoke. She operated under the premise that talking would scare away the fish. Rather than making her squirm, she relaxed into the silence. And the more she relaxed the more air it seemed she could draw into her lungs.

She caught two fish. Mitch identified them,

but one of them was too small so they tossed it back. Mitch caught three fish—a tailor and two mullet. He turned to her with a grin that cracked her chest open wide. 'Guess what we're having for lunch?'

She stared, and then her throat thickened. She had to swallow before she could speak. 'Fish and chips?'

'The very one.'

Her favourite.

She'd never have fish and chips again without thinking of this day. And him.

'Why are you being so nice to me?' she blurted out. She didn't mean to break the summer-holiday spell, but she couldn't hold the question back.

He gazed at her and she couldn't read a single thought in his face.

'I mean you could've just left me to my own devices, stayed out of my way as much as you could while still keeping an eye on me. But you haven't. You've tried to take my mind off the fact that someone wants to hurt me. You've tried to give me the holiday I'm missing out on. You didn't have to do any of that.'

He looked away. 'I'm enjoying it too.'

'I know, but it's not what I asked.'

He turned back and, while she couldn't make out his thoughts, she recognised the turbulence in his eyes. She could let the matter drop. She could say it didn't matter and that she wouldn't look a gift horse in the mouth, but she didn't want to. She wanted to know why.

And why do you want to know that?

Without warning, the blood started to thunder in her ears. Mitch lifted one broad shoulder. 'On Saturday it was because I felt bad that you were in this situation.'

Pity. She tried to keep her face unreadable.

'And you can add guilt to the mix when I found out about your father…about how I'd read that situation so wrong.'

She bit back a sigh.

His gaze speared to hers.

'I like you, Tash.'

Her heart threatened to pummel its way out of her chest.

'I liked you eight years ago. I wish I'd—'

He broke off and stared out to sea.

'You used me eight years ago.'

'Yes, I did. And I'm sorry.'

She lifted a shoulder; let it drop. 'I believe you. I'm not looking for another apology, but what's to say you're not using me again now?' And that, just like eight years ago, he wasn't doing his best to make her fall for him, hook, line and sinker?

Hook, line and sinker? And here they were, fishing. That'd almost be funny except she'd lost her funny bone.

They'd both set their rods to one side. With nothing to encumber him, Mitch leaned in close, trapping her against warm rock. She stared at a tanned forearm and her gaze made a slow salacious survey along it, taking in the strong wrist, the dusting of light hairs along a lean contoured muscle and further up to biceps that flexed with calculated accommodation. Her stomach fluttered. It threatened to dissolve when she studied shoulders so broad they'd withstand storms and gales and other catastrophes. 'Do you know how revealing your question is, Tash?'

She made herself frown. *Keep breathing. Don't forget to keep breathing.*

'It sounds as if you want to trust me, but are afraid I'll take advantage of you again.'

His words wove around her, pregnant with promise and charged with a sensuality she wanted to fall into. She did want to trust him. It might make her an idiot, but…

He leaned in even closer and she could smell the warmth of the sun on his skin. He removed his sunglasses and the lick of his desire flicked along her veins as she gazed into eyes too blue surely to contain lies. The urge to drag his lips down to hers swelled inside her until she could barely think of anything else. She ached to kiss him as a fully-grown woman. She craved to touch him, to taste him, to push him beyond the couple of fleeting kisses they'd shared eight years ago.

When he reached out to remove her sunglasses she snapped back to herself. Very gently she shook her head and pushed him away.

She'd had a lot of practice at pushing men away—it was her default position—but it had never been this hard before.

A sigh eased out of him, but he moved out of her personal space and back to his piece of rock. It was all she could do not to heave out a sigh too.

'I don't know how to answer your question, Tash. At least, not in a way that could convince you I'm not trying to use you to gain inside information on Rick.'

They were both silent.

'I'm not part of the team currently investigating him. My boss knew I had this place and knew we all had a history. I suspect he wanted me out of the way.'

Interesting.

'But, other than the preliminary questions I asked you about Rick on Monday, I haven't mentioned him again. Maybe that'll speak more loudly in my favour than any other assurances I can give you.'

She moistened her lips. 'But you're giving me those assurances as well?'

He held her gaze. 'Yes.'

'There is something you ought to know about Rick.' The blood thundered in her ears. 'He wasn't the drug supplier eight years ago. He took the rap for someone else. And, before you ask, I'm not at liberty to tell you who that someone is.'

His head snapped back. His eyes narrowed, instantly alert. 'Are you being threatened or blackmailed by this person?'

'No, but I made a promise.'

'Do you think this has a bearing on the current case?'

She shook her head. 'I just think it's something you ought to know, that's all.'

His gaze sharpened. 'Why? Especially if you won't tell me the truth so amends can be made to Rick.'

'Why?' She flung out a hand. 'Because, Mitch, you keep getting Rick wrong and it seems to me that it's in my best interests if this time you get him right.'

'Oh, my God!' Tash groaned her pleasure. 'These are the best fish and chips I have ever eaten in my life!'

That sparked the beginning of a smile from Mitch, but she'd hoped for more. Since their conversation about Rick, he'd been quiet. Too quiet.

He was probably mulling everything over and trying to determine whether she could possibly be telling him the truth. And, if so, who on earth could be responsible instead.

Mitch was a good cop, but she and Rick had protected Cheryl well. She doubted his suspicion would fall there. And she was glad about that. She and Rick might've had things hard, but Cheryl had had them so much harder.

'Mitch?'

He barely glanced up.

She waved a hand in front of his face. 'Can you stop working and enjoy the day and this place the way you've been trying to get me to?'

'But—'

'No buts. Let sleeping dogs lie. Believe me, it's for the best.'

Cheryl had gone on to make something of herself. She'd always been smart and she'd worked hard. That shouldn't all become forfeit now because of one stupid youthful mistake.

'Who are you to decide that?'

He glared. She blinked, and then she swallowed. 'So…so you believe me then?'

He swiped a hand through the air. 'I don't know.'

They sat outside at the camp table and the conversation seemed at odds with the beauty of their surroundings. 'I shouldn't have mentioned it.' She should've kept her mouth firmly shut.

'You should've *mentioned it* eight years ago.' His words emerged low and savage.

She responded as if bitten. 'What do you care, huh? You got to close the case! You got the kudos and the promotion and the satisfaction of being considered the brightest new spark on the force. *You* got everything you wanted.'

He shot to his feet. 'I happen to believe in the law and justice!' His chair crashed to the ground. 'I want the right people charged with the crimes they're responsible for! I'm not after quick fixes. I'm after the truth. What right did you or Rick or any of the others that you ran around with back then have to pervert the course of justice?'

His anger sparked hers and she shot to her feet too. 'What right?' she spat. 'What right? Truth and justice were myths where I came from. Where was this Utopian ideal when my father was laying into me with his fists? Where was it when Rick's mother was selling her body on the street?'

'You never told me about your situation! You never told anyone.'

But the evidence had been there if he or any of the authorities had looked harder.

'As for Rick's mother...' He rubbed the back

of his neck. 'It's why social services placed him with his grandmother.'

'Oh, for heaven's sake, Mitch! His grandmother was turning tricks too.'

His jaw slackened and all of the fight drained out of her. 'We had no faith in a system that had done us no favours.'

The anger seemed to bleed out of him then too. 'Did you ever really trust me, Tash?'

'I trusted you, just not what you stood for.'

'And what if that's one and the same thing?'

She righted her chair and sat heavily. 'That's what I'm afraid of.'

Mitch righted his chair and sat too. Their half-finished lunch seemed to mock her. She suspected his appetite had gone the way of hers.

'I don't expect you to understand us or our motives back then. Unless you've grown up that way...' She trailed off. She was glad Mitch hadn't grown up like she had. She wished she believed in truth and justice the way he did.

'You think my life has been a bed of roses?'

He gave a laugh she didn't understand and her chin came up. 'I wouldn't have a clue. How could

I? You never talked about your childhood. So you can lose the tone and the attitude, buster.'

Amazingly, he almost smiled and she found an answering tug deep down inside her. She did her best to resist it.

'I moved to the Western suburbs of Sydney with my grandparents when I was twelve.'

She held her breath to see if he would continue.

'And you're right, I didn't experience the poverty or the poor education or lack of health benefits or any of the other things that were rife throughout the area and made your life so difficult.'

She hadn't known Mitch until he'd returned from his police training, when all the girls in her year at high school had declared him the hottest thing on two legs.

'Where had you lived before that?'

'A small rural town in northern New South Wales. King is my mother's maiden name. My grandparents changed my name by deed poll when I came to live with them.'

She sat back, a chill chasing its way down her back. 'Why?'

'To protect my privacy. To give me a chance to start over.'

She stared at him. Her skin tightened at the grim set of his face. 'To start over from what?'

His face froze into an unfamiliar immobility. 'When I was twelve my father murdered my mother.'

The words were weighted all wrong and it took a moment for their meaning to hit her. When they did she swayed and braced one hand against the table to prevent herself from falling. The table tipped dangerously and for a moment everything on it was in danger of sliding into her lap.

What?

What!

She slammed her other hand down to the table to steady it, to steady herself, to counter the painful pounding of her heart. She wanted to ask him to repeat what he'd just said. Had he really said…? A gaping hole billowed in her stomach. She opened her mouth… But what could she say? There were no words adequate to sweep away the horror of his revelation and what he'd been forced to live with.

I was hungry to save the world.

He shrugged and a vice tightened about her ribs. Mitch hadn't wanted to save the world. He'd just wanted to save his mum. Twelve years old! Her hands clenched. She bit back tears. 'Mitch, I'm so sorry. That's…it's…I'm so sorry.'

How did someone overcome such a thing? The grudge she'd held against him for the last eight years suddenly seemed petty and trivial. The remnants of it disappeared without so much as a *poof*!

She adjusted her cap and tried to rein in the racing of her heart. 'I think it's amazing—everything you've achieved—after that kind of trauma.' It was the kind of thing that could ruin a person's life forever.

'It's a testament to my grandparents' love and care.'

His face had shuttered against her. 'Do you hate him?' she whispered. 'Your father?'

'I did for a long time, but not any more.' He lifted his chin and his gaze was almost a physical brush against her skin, like the soft breeze that danced between them. She breathed in the scent of salt and sun-warmed grasses. Listened to the rhythmic whoosh of the waves on the beach. Very slowly it eased the pounding of her pulse.

They stared at each other for what seemed like a very long time. 'I feel as if I'm finally starting to understand you,' she said.

'Is that a good thing?'

It wasn't necessarily comfortable, but... 'I think so. I can see now why becoming—being—a policeman is so important to you, why it's a vocation and not just a job.' He wanted to protect people like his mother. 'I can see why truth and justice are concepts you want to believe in and uphold.'

Her thoughts started to swirl every which way like a beer pulled too hard that became all froth. One thought eventually detached itself and demanded her attention. She sat on her hands and ground her toes against the rubber of her flip-flops. 'I owe you an apology.'

His lips flattened against his teeth. 'I don't want your pity, Tash. It's not why I told you my story.'

'Pity isn't my primary emotion at the moment.' She shifted on her chair. 'Shame is.' She held up a hand to stall him when he leaned towards her. 'I know that's not what you intended either so cool down. Your story has helped me put what happened between us into perspective. It's obvious I've held onto my grudge and sense of injury for far too long. I thought you were some black-hearted, double-crossing, holier-than-thou hypocrite who'd do anything for a promotion. It was easier to blame you than…than to take a long hard look at myself.'

'I did deceive you,' he said quietly. 'I led you on, gained your trust, let you think I was interested in you.'

'Yes, but you were motivated by much purer motives than I've ever attributed to you before. You weren't a cold-hearted traitor hell-bent on being fast-tracked through the force for your own glory. You were just like me—trying to do the best you could with the resources you had available.'

She couldn't say the realisation left her feeling lighter, but it did leave her feeling cleaner.

He was silent for a moment. 'Are you trying to tell me you've forgiven me?'

She smiled then. 'I'm trying to say that, if you're amenable, I'd like to be friends.'

Really? Had she really just offered Mitch

friendship? She waited for panic and regrets to rip through her, to bathe her in a cold sweat, for a retraction to form on her lips. But none of that happened.

Those blue eyes surveyed her steadily. 'You sure about that?'

She moistened her lips and nodded. 'I'm sure.'

Mitch's gazed snagged on her lips and his eyes darkened. An answering heat swam through her, threatening to drown her, and *that* thickened her throat with panic. 'Friendship is all I'm offering, Mitch.'

He snapped back to himself. 'Of course.'

She shrugged. 'I mean…'

'What?' he barked.

'You might not want that.' He might have enough friends.

'I want.'

The way he said that made her swallow. 'It might not work.'

He folded his arms. 'Why not?'

She couldn't think of a single reason. She glared at him. 'Fine. We're friends then.'

He grinned and her blood leapt. 'Have you ever snorkelled, Tash?'

She shook her head.

'Then you're in for a treat this afternoon.'

The snorkelling was fun.

Once Tash managed to drag her attention from Mitch's powerfully muscled body, that was.

After the snorkelling he left her alone to swim and loaf on the beach with a book. Eventually, though, he called her up to the cabin.

'What's this?' she asked, surveying the sand-wiches cut into small triangles and arranged on plates, the cheese and crackers, and the two generous slices of the cake they'd baked and iced yesterday. 'Are we having a campers' version of high tea?'

'Neither of us finished our lunch and I want you to keep your strength up for this evening's entertainment.'

This evening's entertainment! If he'd said that to her while they'd been snorkelling she'd have gulped water and sunk.

He glanced around at her and a laugh snorted out of him. 'I could only wish!'

Heat stampeded into her face. His words should've put her mind at rest, only... Actually, her mind was fine; it was her body that wanted to squirm and scratch and find some outlet to soothe the restlessness coursing through it.

'Have something to eat, Tash. You must be hungry after all of that exercise.'

She reached for a sandwich and devoured it. Mitch matched her sandwich for sandwich, bite for bite, and she couldn't help wondering if he'd make love with the same enthusiasm. He caught her gaze and, to her horror, she suspected her conjecture was plain for him to read. Her heart flattened and then pounded so hard it almost winded her. 'I, uh…this is the best cake that was ever baked, you know?'

'That was never in question.'

'What are we doing this evening? What are these entertainments you're talking about?'

'Never you mind. I expect you'll want a shower first, but all will be revealed soon enough.'

Right. 'So it doesn't involve swimming or water sports?'

'Nope. There'll be a bit of walking involved, but not a lot. You might want to cover your legs and wear sneakers.'

'Okay.'

She sliced off a piece of cheese and ate it before declaring she couldn't eat another thing. She drained her bottle of water and then headed for the shower.

When she finally joined Mitch again in the main living area, the salt washed from her hair and body, she wore a pair of cargo pants and a T-shirt. The only covered shoes she had with her were her work boots so she tugged those on. They probably looked incongruous with the rest of her outfit, but the warmth in Mitch's eyes informed her she looked just fine.

Better than fine, in fact.

She swallowed and tried not to dwell on that.

Oh, dear Lord, she needed a cold shower.

You just had one!

Mitch wore a pair of shorts, a sand-coloured polo shirt that somehow made the blue of his eyes all the more vivid, and tennis shoes without socks. He looked just as tempting now as he had on the beach in his board shorts. Her heart thumped. Her mouth dried. There was no point denying it. A big part of her wished this evening's entertainments involved staying in, lighting candles and—

'Ready for another adventure?'

She snapped to, straightened and nodded. 'Sure am.'

He ushered her outside, settling the backpack on his shoulder. She tried to not let her gaze linger on those shoulders.

'So what are we doing? Where are we going?' She desperately needed to move her mind to safer channels.

'We're going for a walk.'

The rest of her questions dried on her tongue when he reached across and took her hand and led her along a track into the eucalypt forest. She stared at their linked hands and something started to burn low in her belly.

'You uh…worried I'm going to trip over?'

He sent her a grin. 'Nah, I just want to hold your hand, Tash. Is that a problem?'

She was sure it should be, but she found herself shaking her head and mouthing a silent, 'No.'

'Good.'

So, you going to let him kiss you next? Make love with you because you sure as heck don't have a problem with those things either, do you?

She waved a hand in front of her face. *Quiet!*

Mitch squeezed her hand and then released it. 'We'll have to go in single file from here for a bit, and we'll need to be as quiet as we can.'

She opened her mouth, but after a second closed it again and just nodded. He wanted to surprise her and she found she didn't want to spoil his fun. When he set off she followed, curling her fingers into her palm and holding it against her chest.

Late afternoon light filtered down from the heights of the trees. Birdsong rang in the treetops. She identified the laughter of a kookaburra and the warbling of three magpies, recognised the noisy miners as they darted among the branches and caught a flash of a blue wren in amongst the dense scrub. The sound of cicadas stop-started in their strange musical round.

She loved this time of day and she allowed the sounds and scents of the forest to filter through and relax her. They walked for somewhere close to ten minutes, she guessed, before Mitch stopped. He held a finger up to his lips and then pointed to the clearing ahead. He eased forward and she crept along after him. He stopped again and motioned for her to ease up beside him. And that was when she saw it. Them.

Kangaroos.

Actually, they were wallabies—the kangaroo's smaller cousin—but she wasn't all that concerned with semantics as she crouched beside Mitch, mouth agape, and watched them.

There had to be at least a dozen of them grazing in contented clusters in the clearing. Gripping Mitch's arm, she grinned at him and pointed to a joey in its mother's pouch. He pointed to another one.

She couldn't remember the last time she'd seen kangaroos—or wallabies—in the wild. She stared, drinking in their oddness—their long ears and tiny front paws, the way they balanced on strong tails and the cute pointed faces of the joeys. Sometimes it wasn't a face but a flash of a hind leg stretching from the pouch.

At the same time and on a more primitive level, she relished the muscled strength of Mitch as she leaned into him, his shoulder and arm warm and reassuring where it pressed against hers.

A tiny breeze danced up then and the largest buck stretched up, sniffing the air. Without warning, as one they all leapt off into the deeper gloom of the forest.

She stood and stretched. She couldn't wipe the grin from her face. 'That was really something!'

He grinned back. 'Thought you'd enjoy it. I know it's not the same as visiting a wildlife park where you'd get a chance to feed and pet them, but—'

'It's better,' she said, and she meant it.

The sun had started to set and the shadows in the forest started to deepen. Mitch swung the backpack off his shoulder. Was her phone still in there? She shrugged, not much caring if it was or wasn't. He rummaged in its depths before handing her a bottle of water and producing a torch. He swung its light into the trees surrounding them. He moved around from tree to tree for probably two or three minutes before he found what he was looking for.

'There.' He drew her in closer to his side so she could follow the line of his arm and the beam of light.

'Oh!' she gasped. She took the torch from him and moved closer to the tree. 'A koala!' She stared and stared. It didn't move. It rested in the fork of the tree, obviously asleep. Apparently, koalas slept for around twenty hours a day. She refused to take her eyes from it, afraid it'd disappear. 'I've never seen a koala in the wild before.'

'It's something, isn't it?'

He'd moved up behind her and his heat surrounded her, his breath disturbing the hair at her temple. Pinpricks of awareness tiptoed up her spine, one vertebra at a time. She swallowed. She should say something to try and dispel the awareness before it sunk its claws into her any deeper. 'Is there a cuter animal on the planet?'

'I don't know if you think they're cuter...' she heard the smile in his voice '...but if you're happy to sit on that log over there for a while the possums will show themselves soon.'

She didn't move towards the log. She turned to him instead. He mightn't have been able to give her surfboarding lessons, but he had given her the surf. Paddleboats had been out of the question, but he'd taken her kayaking. Takeaway pizza might've been off the menu but he'd found a way to give her fish and chips. And now he'd shared the magic of the local wildlife with her.

He'd tried to give her everything she'd wanted from a holiday. What was more, he'd made her forget the malice awaiting her at home. 'You've given me the most perfect couple of days, Mitch.'

'I'm glad.'

This man had been through so much pain and suffering himself and all he wanted to do was ease it in others. How could she have misjudged him so badly? She couldn't tell if his eyes had darkened or if that was the night deepening. 'You've made me forget the bad stuff.'

'That was the plan.'

She moved closer and she suddenly felt more alive than she ever had before. 'I don't think I will ever be able to thank you properly for that.' The torch slipped from her fingers to the ground at her feet. She lifted her hands, flattened them against his chest. She couldn't mistake the way his breath hitched or the way his heart pounded against her palm.

'Tash.'

Her name growled from him and she had a feeling he'd meant it as a warning, but it came out as a caress. When she stood on tiptoe to touch her lips to his, his hands shot to her shoulders as if to put her away from him, but his lips opened to hers and their tongues danced. He tasted of the sea and summer and shady glades and she forgot who was kissing who as their bodies crashed together, needing the contact and seeking more.

Eventually he held her away from him, breathing hard as if he'd been sprinting. 'That's not the way to thank me, Tash.'

She gripped his forearms to try and find her balance. 'It stopped being a thank you after the first kiss.'

'You said this was a bad idea.'

'When?'

'This afternoon you said friendship was all that was on offer. This morning you backed away from a kiss.'

The words emerged through gritted teeth and she could see how tightly he held himself in check. She sympathised. She hadn't wanted him with this kind of physical ferocity eight years ago. She could see now how careful he'd been with her back then. If he'd chosen to, he could've created this kind of heat in her. She wouldn't have been ready for it. She wouldn't have known how to deal with it. But there wasn't a doubt in her mind that she'd have succumbed to it.

He hadn't let that happen then, but she was more than ready for it to happen now. 'I must've had rocks in my head.' Her fingers curled into the material of his shirt. 'Besides, I understand it's a woman's prerogative to change her mind.'

He groaned.

She frowned. 'You think it's a bad idea?'

'I'm supposed to be guarding you, protecting you.'

'Correction—you're making sure I'm out of harm's way. You said the danger wouldn't follow us here.'

'It won't, but—'

'Then the idea that you need to be hyper-vigilant is nonsense and you know it.'

He didn't say anything.

'You know there is something that could make my holiday truly unforgettable.'

'What's that?'

'A holiday fling.'

He swore. It came out sounding like an endearment.

'I know most people consider me a tough customer with attitude to burn. That translates in some circles as me being considered something of a...*bad* girl.'

His eyes widened. His nostrils flared.

'The fact of the matter is the opposite is true.' The very opposite, in fact, but she had no intention of sharing that.

His body was beautiful and utterly beguiling and everything inside her arched towards it, aching to explore it.

His eyes gleamed in the light of the rising moon. 'Are you telling me, Tash, that you want to do something wild and reckless?'

She smiled back at him. 'I'm glad to see you've finally got with the programme, Officer King.'

CHAPTER SEVEN

THEY MADE IT back to the cabin in record time.

No sooner had they slammed the door behind them than Mitch backed her up against it, his lips hot and hungry on hers. A faint circle of yellow light pooled around the lamp on the kitchen bench, and moonlight filtered through the windows to wink off the framed prints on the walls and a couple of glittery book spines in the bookcase.

The rough wood of the door jabbed into her back. Slipping her arms from around his neck, she leant them against his chest and walked him backwards into the room, not breaking the lip lock, enjoying the feel and taste of him too much.

One of his hands snaked around her backside, pulling her hard against him. She gasped as the heat in her spread further, the need…and the thrill. Her knees started to buckle and he lowered them to the ground with more speed than grace so that she straddled him. Their noses collided, her elbow hit the ground with a crack and Mitch swore as something of his—an ankle or shin—connected with the hard leg of the coffee table.

She ignored it all. She wanted skin on skin contact. Now!

With a growl she bunched up his T-shirt and ran her hands over his stomach and chest. Mitch moaned, his muscles clenching beneath her fingertips. In the dim light his muscled flesh gleamed. She ran her hands over him again. He jerked beneath her touch, his eyes glittering.

She did that? Created that need, that fever in him? Her?

She ran her hands lower, dipping them beneath the waistband—the tantalisingly low waistband—of his shorts and his body bucked beneath her touch. She grinned. She sat up straighter and tossed her hair.

'Tash,' he warned.

'I want you to take your shirt off,' she commanded.

He rose up on his elbows to survey her. It pushed the bulge in his shorts more firmly against the juncture of her thighs.

'Oh!' She swayed. She had to swallow, twice, to clear her head.

He grinned that slow crooked grin and her pulse rate ratcheted up another notch. 'So that's how you want to play it, huh?'

With another man she suspected self-conscious-ness would've crippled her by now, but not with Mitch. The fire in his eyes didn't leave any room for that kind of nonsense.

Should she tell him…?

She hitched up her chin. 'You have a problem with that?'

In one swift motion he pulled his shirt over his head and tossed it to one side. She didn't bother watching to see where it fell. She was too busy taking in the broad sweep of his shoulders and the depth of his chest, the way the muscles in his upper arms bulged and the lean tapering of his stomach that had more definition than a dic-tionary. And then she let her hands follow her gaze—slowly and comprehensively. She wanted to know every inch of this man.

His hands snaked under her shirt, playing havoc with her concentration, and she batted them away. 'No touching!'

He grinned and her blood heated up so fast it almost bubbled. 'At least take your shirt off too.' His voice came out like warm honey, flowing over her in promised sweetness. 'It's only fair.'

She considered that. She didn't care about fair. All she wanted to do was drive Mitch crazy in the same way he'd driven her crazy since they'd first met. That was why she pulled her shirt over her head and tossed it one way. It was why she unclasped her bra and tossed it the other. And it was why she squirmed in what she hoped was a seductive way, thrusting her breasts forward, nipples peaking as the grin dropped away from his face and he moistened his lips. 'You're beautiful,' he said, his voice a hoarse groan in the semi-darkness.

Astride him like this, she felt beautiful.

He reached for her again, but she wrapped her fingers around his wrists and pushed them down to the ground beside his head. 'All my life I've been a good girl.'

She didn't expect him to believe her. She didn't expect anyone to believe her. She'd always acted as if she'd been around the block a few times, but it simply wasn't the truth. Would Mitch run for the hills if he knew she was a virgin? She wasn't taking that chance. Maybe he wouldn't even notice.

She stared into his eyes. 'Just once I want to act out and be the bad girl, be…depraved.'

Pushing his hands down had brought her face close to his. Those mesmerising blue eyes locked to hers. 'Have you been reading *Fifty Shades*, Tash?'

Just the way he said it made her feel deliciously racy. 'What if I have?'

'Would you like me to spank you?' He lifted his head and his lips brushed her ear as he spoke, his breath stirred the hair at her temple and her nipples started to ache. 'Should I get my hand-cuffs?'

'If you do I'll brain you with them.' But her voice came out on nothing more than a whisper of breath. The low rumble in his throat told her he didn't believe her.

He lifted his head again and slid a warm moist tongue across one of her nipples. She stiffened as if electrified, every nerve in her body springing to life. The knot in her stomach grew.

'I said no touch—'

He took the nipple all the way into his mouth and suckled. She arched against him with a gasp that was half moan. Nothing had ever felt so good, so urgent!

In one fluid motion he sat up, his mouth never leaving her breast, one hand between her shoulder blades to pull her more firmly against him while his free hand cupped her other breast, the thumb moving back and forth until she thought she might drown in sensation.

Her breath came in short sharp pants. She arched against his mouth. She arched against his groin. Both of them had grown slick with perspiration.

'You know what I think?' He pressed hot moist kisses to her neck, his finger flipping open the fly button of her cargo pants as if he'd done so a thousand times before.

'What's that?' she panted.

'What you really need…'

He didn't really mean to spank her, did he? It might get her hot to talk about it but she'd run a mile if he tried it. She pushed away from him to stare into his eyes. He brushed the hair off her face. 'What you really need, Natasha Buckley…'

His use of her full name in his desire-thickened murmur made her shiver. He ran his fingers down the side of her breasts and she had to catch her lip between her teeth to stop from crying out.

'...is to lose control.'

She did?

'You repress too much, little Miss Wound-Too-Tight, but not tonight.'

'I am not—'

His mouth captured a nipple again.

She moaned when deft, knowing fingers did things that had never been done to her before.

'You were saying?' he said lazily against her mouth, before rolling them both over.

Her knee hit the coffee table and his elbow cracked on something. 'When I was seventeen and fantasizing about making love with you, it wasn't like this.'

'No?' He stared down at her as she tried to unpin her hair from beneath her.

'Everything was smooth and cool and graceful. There was no sweat, no bumping of noses and...'

He cupped her breast and ran a thumb back and forth over her nipple. 'Was there any of this?'

She swallowed. 'Of course.' But back then

there'd been nothing so raw and elemental as the sensations crowding her now. She hadn't even dreamt of such a thing. 'But please, Mitch, I'm going to be black and blue tomorrow.'

'You're going to be very, *very* satisfied tomorrow,' he promised, a glint in his eye.

Hauling himself to his feet, he picked her up and strode towards the bedroom.

Mitch stared up at the ceiling, his fingers idly running up and down Tash's back. He loved the feel of her bare skin against him, her warm breath on his chest.

They hadn't spoken.

Yet.

He hadn't opened his mouth because making love with Tash had been so intense it'd rocked the very fabric of his world. He wasn't sure how she felt. He knew he'd given her pleasure, but...

He glanced down at her. 'You okay?'

He could feel her smile against him. She snuggled closer. 'I'm better than okay.'

He let out a careful breath and closed his eyes for a moment. 'Why didn't you tell me?' he asked quietly.

She stilled. He tightened an arm about her so she wouldn't move away. 'You could tell, then?'

'Uh huh.'

She'd given him her virginity. Why? Did that mean something? If she'd been holding onto it for this long then it had to mean something, didn't it?

He frowned at the ceiling. 'You should've told me.'

'Why?'

He moved away a little to stare down into her face. 'Because I'd have been gentler, more careful.'

'I don't have any complaints.'

That didn't answer the question.

'And I didn't want to give you an excuse to stop.'

'I'm not sure I could've stopped,' he was honest enough to admit.

She'd given him her virginity and, while he couldn't explain it, she was now burned onto his soul. He had a feeling that should frighten him, but it didn't. What worried him was the way he wanted to beat his chest and shout out a Tarzan cry like some primitive being.

'Would you have believed me?'

He stiffened until he recognised there was no accusation in her voice. 'It's a surprise,' he admitted. 'But I'd have believed you.'

She lifted up on one elbow to stare down into his face. 'Did it affect your pleasure? Was it not—'

'You rocked, Tash. We rocked. I can't remember the last time I…' He trailed off. He couldn't remember the last time making love had touched him so deeply. 'It was amazing.'

Her smile squeezed something tight in his chest.

'Rest now.' He pressed her head back to his shoulder, wrapped an arm securely about her. She'd given him her virginity. It *had* to mean something.

When Mitch woke the next morning, he knew exactly what the previous night meant. It meant that he and Tash belonged together. He knew that with every fibre that made him who he was. And he needed to make sure they were on the same page about that.

Tash wasn't in bed with him, but the scent of coffee told him she wasn't far.

He grinned, suddenly flooded with more energy than he could ever remember—it coursed through every atom until he zinged with it, floated with it and felt as if he could conquer the world. He swooped out into the main room of the cabin, pulled on a pair of tracksuit pants, and a quick glance out of the door told him Tash was down on the beach. He made a flask of tea, grabbed a packet of biscuits and headed down to the beach.

She turned before his feet hit the sand, a smile lifting her lips. As he made his way across to where she sat, her eyes made a slow—and comprehensive—appraisal of his body, and the gleam that lit them nearly made him stumble. Then he had to fight the urge to run to her, sticking his chest out and beating it caveman-style. And he was glad—*very* glad—he hadn't bothered with a shirt. He wished she hadn't bothered with a shirt either. No matter. He meant to divest her of it as soon as possible.

'Good morning.' Her voice held a breathy edge that made him hard in an instant.

He dropped a kiss to her lips—quick, light,

playful—and then fell down beside her. 'I come bearing breakfast.'

She glanced at the biscuits and then arched an eyebrow. 'I'm going to need more than that to keep me going today.'

He nearly tossed the flask and biscuits to one side to take her then and there on the sand under the sun. He pulled back at the last moment. She was probably sore after last night. And they had plenty of time. They had the rest of their lives. 'I'll cook up something more substantial in a bit,' he promised. 'I wanted to talk.'

She trailed a finger along his inner thigh. 'It's not what I had in mind.'

He captured her hand, kissed her fingers. The hunger in her eyes, the laughter and warmth in her face, told him she was in as deep as he was. His heart soared. 'Last night was incredible.'

'You won't get any arguments from me on that head.'

'It might sound like a cliché, Tash, but last night meant something to me. Something big.'

The amber in her eyes turned gold.

'We've only been out here three days—four

counting today—but I feel as if my whole life has been turned on its head.'

She stared at him and then finally nodded. 'Me too.'

He kissed her fingers again and then released her to pour them mugs of tea. He tore open the biscuits, ravenous.

She took one and nibbled the edge. 'I can't help feeling things have been moving a whole lot faster than they should be.'

'Or perhaps they're moving at exactly the right pace.'

She'd given him her virginity. And he knew what that meant—she was his and he was going to love and protect her for the rest of their lives. He'd let her down once. He wasn't letting her down again.

'I lay awake for a long time last night, thinking.' He'd felt alive and contented—whole in a way he hadn't thought possible. When his father had killed his mother it had fractured something inside him. Last night Tash had put him back together. He turned to her. 'We belong together, you and me.' Nothing had ever made more sense to him than that.

Her hand froze halfway to her mouth with her biscuit. She stared at him, her jaw slack. He didn't blame her for her surprise. The realisation had shocked him too.

'Look, I thought about it long and hard. You want to hear my plan?'

She moistened her lips. 'Okay.'

He pulled in a breath. 'This is what I think we should do. When we get back to Sydney, you should move in with me.' His house was in a nicer suburb than Tash's. 'You can give up your job.'

He hated the thought of her slaving away behind the bar of the Royal Oak. 'That pub is in a rough neighbourhood and I hate the thought of you being subjected to any kind of violence or threat.' He pulled in a breath. 'You can go back to school if you want.' She could train for a better job, a safer job. Eventually they'd marry and have a couple of kids. It'd be perfect. But that could wait. He didn't want to rush her.

'Have you completely lost your mind?'

Tash struggled to her feet, spraying sand all over the biscuits. The only reason the tea didn't go flying was that Mitch put a hand out to steady the flask.

'I'm not going back to school! What on earth would I want to do that for?'

He spread his hands. 'It was just a suggestion and—'

'I'm not giving up my job!'

'It puts you in danger!' He shot upright too.

'Garbage! I can handle myself at work.' She poked him in the chest. 'I like my job. I'm good at it. That means something to me.'

His face twisted in frustration. 'But—'

'And it's not as dangerous as your job!'

'That's different!'

'How?' she shot back. 'You like it, don't you? You're good at it, aren't you?' She folded her arms. 'Are you going to volunteer to give it up in this cosy little scenario of yours?'

He scowled. 'Of course not.'

'I'm *not* moving in with you, Mitch.'

She had a feeling she was ticking each of these points off in the wrong order. 'We've known each other for all of three days!' Things never worked out as rosily as Mitch was picturing. He knew that!

'It's not about how long you know someone. It's

about how well you know them.' He thumped his chest. *'In here.* It's having the courage to follow through on your convictions.'

He was calling her a coward? She clenched her hands so hard she shook. 'I'll give you convictions! What you want to do is set me up in a pretty cage, but a cage all the same. And I know that has to do with how powerless you felt about your mum, but I am not letting anybody take away my freedom like that. I'm an adult and I have the right to make my own decisions. I know what it feels like to have no power and I'm not going back to that again.'

They stared at each other, both breathing hard.

She recalled her heartbreak eight years ago and fear clogged her throat. She slashed a hand through the air. 'What on earth has got into you? Yesterday you were a reasonable human being. Today you're acting like some…caveman!'

He dragged a hand down his face.

'I thought it was women who started building pipe dreams and happy-ever-afters after sex, not men.'

He stared back at her stonily. 'You were a virgin.'

She adjusted her stance. 'So?'

'So it has to mean something. You're twenty-five, for heaven's sake. To have waited this long...'

She had to stifle the frustrated scream that rose in her throat, but behind it shivered a twist of fear. 'It doesn't mean anything!'

She stomped down to the water's edge to kick as much water in the air as she could—dreadfully childish but satisfying all the same. She stomped back to where Mitch stood. 'I'll tell you what it means, Mitch. I'm a prude!'

His jaw dropped. 'The hell you are.'

She chafed her arms, turning to stare back out at the water. 'Maybe not anymore.' And that was a relief to know. 'I...' She had to swallow. 'I don't remember my parents ever being nice to one another.' She sure as heck couldn't imagine them making love the way she and Mitch had last night.

It has to mean something.

Her scalp prickled. Her throat threatened to close over. 'There weren't really any role models for me to look up to in that way when I was growing up. Rick's mother and grandmother horrified me. I couldn't imagine...' She shuddered and suddenly he was standing beside her. He didn't touch her, but his presence helped unclench something inside her.

'When I was fifteen, a girl at school got pregnant. Her boyfriend dumped her and her mother kicked her out. She received social security benefits but every time I saw her she looked thinner and dirtier. She died of a drug overdose and her baby went into foster care. Another friend from school was sexually abused by her father.'

Mitch let forth with a curse.

'Precisely.'

They both stared at the far horizon. Eventually she turned to look at him. 'In my mind, sex has been associated with an awful lot of sordidness.' Especially when she'd been a teenager. 'When I was prepared to risk my heart—which is when I'd have risked my body—I was…hurt. It seemed a crap shoot, sex and romance, and I decided I didn't want any part of it.'

He swore again but this time it was under his breath.

'Nobody warned me about hormones, though. The last twelve months I've been getting…antsy. But I don't meet too many new guys these days.

That's my own fault. I don't go out to places where I can meet them. All the guys who know me don't ask me out any more because I kept turning them down, but these last few days have been...' she reached into the air as if searching for the right word '...a revelation.'

She stared down at her feet, dug her toes in the sand. 'Last night was amazing. I'm glad it happened. But it was just sex.'

Liar.

'The fact I was a virgin doesn't mean anything...except as a sign of my arrested development and teenage hang-ups.' She stared up at him and did what she could to make her face hard and businesslike. 'You hearing me?'

He didn't look at her. 'Loud and clear.'

'I'm going to brush my teeth.'

He didn't follow her so he must've caught her subtext that she wanted to be alone.

She brushed her teeth in time to the panic whirling over and over in her head. She rinsed her mouth and then stomped back to the cabin. Everywhere she looked there was evidence of her encounter with Mitch last night—her bra dangling from a shelf of the bookcase and her T-shirt on the sofa, Mitch's polo shirt under the coffee table.

She grabbed her things and threw them into the bedroom. She grabbed Mitch's shirt and tossed it on the haversack sitting at one end of the sofa. She rubbed her hands up and down the sides of her shorts and turned on the spot.

You just rejected him, you idiot!

No, she hadn't. She'd just made it clear that she wasn't ready to move in with him yet.

You said it was just sex!

She thought back to last night and a dreamy smile built through her. She'd never known that making love could be so…explosive. Or so utterly satisfying.

Or that it could leave her feeling so vulnerable.

She chafed her arms some more and the smile slid off her face. *It was just sex.* She shook her head. It had been a whole lot more than just sex.

But, for heaven's sake, why did Mitch have to go and get all crazy on her and freak her out? Why couldn't he just take things slow—be casual for a bit until she got used to all of this? He'd scared the pants off her and she'd lashed out, said things in a way that… She wrung her hands and searched for something to keep them busy.

Her eyes lit on the backpack abandoned on the floor by the door. She grabbed it, plonked it on the table and proceeded to rinse out and refill the water bottles, set the torch on the bookcase where it was handy for middle-of-the-night calls of nature. She glanced inside to see what else she could tidy up. The phones could stay there. Ditto with the matches and the first aid kit.

A gold wrapper caught her eye. A chocolate bar! Mitch had been holding out on her?

She reached in, seized it—

'What do you think you're doing?'

She swung, her heart in her throat. 'Dammit, Mitch, don't sneak up like that! You trying to give me a heart attack?'

It was good he was here, though. They needed to talk. They needed to get a few things settled.

'I wasn't the one sneaking.' His face darkened. 'That's obviously you.'

She stared at him.

He strode forward and snatched the backpack from the table. 'The minute my back is turned you're on the phone to Rick, right?'

She held up what she had in her hand. 'Choco-late,' she said softly. 'Not a phone.'

He blinked.

'Despite everything I told you, you still believe Rick is guilty, don't you?'

'Jail changes a person.'

A lump of ugliness blocked her throat until she could barely breathe. 'You have a nasty mind sometimes, Mitch, you know that?' She swallowed, forced scorn into her voice. 'Of course I'm going to seduce you, lull you into a false sense of security and then, the moment your guard's down, steal off with my phone and make secret phone calls.'

'Did you try to ring Rick or anyone else?'

'I'm not even going to dignify that with an answer.' She went to swing away, but then swung back. 'But that accusation is very telling. Obviously, if you're worried I'd do that, then Rick can't be out of phone contact like you said.' Her eyes flashed. 'You lied about that.'

'I did.'

He didn't even look remorseful!

'It was easier than telling you that the detectives on the case refused to trust you.'

She folded her arms, her lips twisting as her heart crumpled. 'It's telling on more than one level. After last night, you really think I'd go behind your back like that?'

'What do you mean?' he demanded, his eyes frigid chips of ice. 'Last night was just sex, remember?'

CHAPTER EIGHT

HER BREATH CHOKED in her throat as if he'd slapped her.

Mitch turned grey. 'Tash, I…'

It took an effort to keep her eyes wide and to concentrate on breathing through her nose, counting the breaths to keep the moisture in her eyes from spilling over. *Had her words lacerated his heart like that?*

'I didn't ring Rick. Not that I expect you to believe me.' A black pit of acid rose in her stomach. 'But then trust has never been a strong point between us, has it? If you trusted me, that question would never have arisen. Whatever else you've said this morning, it's obvious now that last night didn't change a thing.'

'If you trusted me you'd have told me you were a virgin.'

He had her there.

The silence between them stretched. This conversation wasn't over, not by a long shot, but she didn't have the heart to continue it for now. She suspected Mitch didn't either. There were too many hurt feelings on both sides.

'I'm going for a swim.' She seized her swimming costume and a towel. 'While you ring your colleagues and inform them of your suspicions.'

He didn't say anything, didn't try to stop her.

And she didn't look back. Not once.

Tash swam.

Yesterday the water had slid like silk against her skin. Today salt and sand stung and chafed.

Yesterday the water had buoyed and supported her and made her feel strong. Today it was all she could do not to sink like a dead, deflated weight.

As she moved through the waves, muscles she'd never known she had ached and protested, screaming out a harsh reminder of her innate weakness for Mitch and all that had happened last night…and how much she'd welcomed it.

Mitch. She hadn't been able to resist him eight years ago and she hadn't been able to resist him last night. Putty—that was all she was where he was concerned. A terrible sense of déjà vu settled around her shoulders, making her arms heavy, her chest heavy, her head heavy.

That gilded cage he'd just presented her with… She choked back something that felt suspiciously like a sob. It'd make her miserable. She closed her eyes and her arms pimpled with gooseflesh. Did he need to put her into that cage for his own happiness, though? Without it, would he be the miserable one instead? She opened her eyes and it didn't matter how fiercely the sun shone, the warmth leached out of the day.

She slapped a hand down onto the water and saltwater flew up to sting her eyes. Why couldn't she have resisted for just another day or two when this whole farce would be over?

She spun and breaststroked into the middle of the bay. If she'd fought against her desire last night she might never have known how amazing making love with Mitch could be. He'd transported her to a place of such pleasure and delight that even now her toes curled just thinking about it. She floated, staring up at a flawless sky, the water a satin caress against her skin, and recalled the way she'd made him moan and shake. Her skin tingled and her muscles quivered and for a moment she felt strong enough to fly.

And then she remembered the way everything had unravelled this morning and she sank. She kicked her head back above water, coughing. All she could see was the way his face had darkened in suspicion when he'd walked through the door and found her with the backpack.

Last night she'd stared into his eyes and had shared her soul. How could he—?

Fool me once, shame on you. Fool me twice, shame on me. 'Fool me thrice...' She pushed her shoulders back and lifted her chin. 'Not going to happen.'

Mitch was waiting for her when she finally returned to shore. Silently he handed her a towel. Just as silently she took it. She took a few steps away from him and turned her back to dry off. She didn't know if he watched her or not, but her back burned as if he did.

'Are you okay?' he finally asked.

'Hunky-dory,' she snapped, tying the towel sarong-style around her waist. 'You?'

He didn't say anything and finally the suspense

grew too much. She turned. She hoped her raised eyebrow hid the raw ache that sawed through her chest.

'I've been better.'

It was something, but nowhere near enough.

'I think I probably owe you an apology.'

She folded her arms and raised both eyebrows.

'I think I've probably misjudged you. If that's the case then I'm sorry.'

I think? Probably? If? Her jaw clenched. Maybe she should just take him apart piece by piece now.

He widened his stance. 'You going to say something?'

She unclenched her jaw to bite out, 'I'm afraid I'm just speechless at such a wholehearted, unreserved apology.'

Red streaked his cheekbones, raw and angry.

She shook her head, just the once. 'I have nothing to say.' The pulse at the base of his jaw jumped and jerked. Swallowing, she dragged her gaze away.

'Then I expect you'll be pleased to know that our time here is done.'

Her eyes flew back to his. The muscles in her arms and legs bunched, but whether in readiness for flight or fight or something altogether differ- ent she didn't know. 'It wouldn't have been over if I'd accepted your apology?'

For a moment his eyes blazed as bright as opals. Her lips twisted in an effort to hide how her pulse leapt. 'You were hoping for some more nookie with the bad girl?'

'It's not like that, Tash.'

She hammered in the last nail and any chance they might've had. 'You know what? I don't much care any more.' There really wasn't anything left to say, anything left to rescue.

Those red slashes turned white. She ignored that. Ignored the pounding of her heart too, to push her shoulders back, lift her chin and settle an indifferent expression on her face. 'I take it Rick has been taken in for questioning?'

He nodded.

'I'd like to see him.'

His face darkened, a clap of thunder in a per- fect summer sky. 'When are you going to stop making a fool of yourself over him?'

'Fool?' Her mouth opened and closed. How could he possibly think she held a torch for Rick after last night?

The same way he could think she'd lie and cheat and sneak his phone this morning, that was how.

She reached down to grasp her towel from where it had started to slip. 'He knows more about friendship than you ever will. When are you going to realise he'd never hurt me? He'd never hurt any woman.'

'Tell that to Dixie Bennett and Leah Manning.'

'Still blinded by prejudice after all this time? You might come across as some kind of moral upholder of all that's good, but beneath the façade you're nothing but a hypocrite.'

'As I said.' His words were clipped. 'We're done here.'

'Halle-bloody-lujah.'

They didn't speak a single word on the way back to Sydney. Tash was careful to keep her hands smooth and relaxed rather than clenched fists in her lap. Mitch had made it known in no uncertain terms that if she wanted to see Rick she could make her way to the police station under her own steam and not his. Apparently he'd take no part in encouraging her folly.

She'd taken one glance at the grim set of his

mouth and had refused to look at him again. She hadn't dignified his dictate with an answer either.

But as they'd driven away from the cabin, with its private beach and memories branded on her brain—and body—her heart burned as it never had before. She would never return to this place and the grief raked away at her, leaving her insides raw and tender, and there was nothing she could do about it.

As they passed from rural tranquillity to the freeway and then the buzz and noise of the city... and finally to her dingy, less-than-salubrious neighbourhood, her thoughts darkened. Mitch didn't even turn the engine off when they reached her house. He leapt out, pulled her suitcase from the boot and set it by her gate. He didn't set so much as a big toe onto her property.

She went to stalk right past him, but he stepped in front of her. 'We are not finished, Tash. I am not going to let you cut me dead the way you have your parents...and probably every other person in your life who has let you down or hurt you. This is not over.'

'That's what you think,' she flung at him to hide her sudden fear and the dread that trickled down her backbone. Her vulnerability to this man scared her senseless. She wanted him gone. *Now.* She stuck out one hip. 'Give my regards to Rick,' she drawled. 'Let him know I'll be there as soon as I can.'

His lips twisted. 'Not going to work.'

What was he talking about?

Snaking his arm around her waist, he pulled her hard up against him. His lips slammed to hers, hard, demanding, insistent. He bit, suckled and laved, and her head spun, her blood sang and all she could do was cling to him and open her mouth to his as and when he demanded it of her. Her breath and her tongue tangled with his until they felt like one. And whole.

And then he released her and she almost fell, except he kept hold of her so she didn't. He swiped his thumb across her swollen bottom lip, a possessive light in his eyes. 'You were a virgin, but that doesn't make you stupid. What we have is amazing and you'll be a fool to walk away from it.'

Her heart pounded. She couldn't think of a single thing to say.

'I didn't fight for you eight years ago, but I'm

not walking away without a fight this time, Tash. I'll see you in the morning. Hopefully by then we'll have both had some time to think things through.'

She watched him walk away and, God forgive her, all she could do was wish tomorrow here already.

It was a full five hours before Detective Glastonbury and his team had finished questioning Rick. But they didn't have enough evidence to hold him and finally Tash was free to take him home.

Before they reached the freedom of the main door, however, Mitch emerged from an office and blocked their way. He stared at her with angry dark eyes that made her swallow and grip her hands in front of her.

Rick folded his arms. 'Well, well, if it isn't Officer King.'

Mitch leaned in close and his scent sparked such a swirl of longing through her it made her dizzy. She had to grip her hands together all the tighter. 'If you harm a single hair on her head, Bradford, I will come after you with everything I've got.'

'If I harm a single hair on her head I'd deserve it,' Rick countered.

Mitch blinked, but his glare didn't abate. 'We're watching you.'

'Message received, loud and clear.'

Tash rolled her eyes and wondered which of them would beat his chest first.

Those devastating eyes turned to her. 'Tomorrow.'

She nodded once. He was right. She couldn't walk away, but she couldn't help thinking this would only end in heartbreak. For both of them. 'Make it mid-morning,' she said to let him know she wasn't wholly against the idea. One way or the other, they needed to clear the air. 'I'll bake a cake.'

'I'm guessing you'd like me to make myself scarce for your big date tomorrow?'

Tash glanced up from the sofa, where she reclined with her brand-spanking-new cookbook. She'd raced out to buy it this afternoon after she and Rick had arrived home, along with a whole load of groceries. She straightened and set her feet on the floor. 'You're more than welcome to stay for cake and coffee if you like.' In fact it would probably be a good idea for Mitch to get to know Rick better. 'But if you found you had some pressing engagement after that I wouldn't mind. Mitch and I have a few things to, uh...' she cleared her throat '...thrash out.'

'I'll be out of here early.'

She bit back a sigh. It'd probably be for the best. 'Thanks, Rick.'

She really wanted to quiz him more about who he thought was behind this spate of violence, who it was that was trying to set him up, but she bit the words back. They'd compared notes already. They'd thrown around ideas, but nothing had stuck.

She knew Rick. She knew how much this would be gnawing away at him. She didn't want to add to that.

He placed his hands behind his head and grinned at her. 'You really going to cook Mitch a cake?'

What on earth had possessed her? She grimaced. 'Yeah.'

He sobered and leaned towards her, elbows on knees. 'Tash, what's going down? What are you hoping for from tomorrow?' He frowned. 'And...'

'And what?'

'What is it you're afraid of?'

She swallowed. He knew her too well, but if she laughed those questions off he'd leave her be. But she didn't want to laugh them off. She wanted to know the answers too. All the same, she did laugh. Not that it held much mirth. 'I can tell you what I'm afraid of. That one's easy. But what I want?' She slammed the cookbook shut and shook her head. She hadn't been able to pin that one down. 'That's proving tough to work out.'

'Then start with the easy stuff.'

She met his gaze. 'You understand that… stuff…happened when Mitch and I were holed up at the cabin, right?' She thought he might roll his eyes at that so she added, 'I'm not just talking about sex.'

She sucked her bottom lip into her mouth, worried at it with her teeth. 'We connected in ways…' She leapt up off the sofa to pace. 'I don't know what you want to call it—emotional, mental, spiritual.' She fell back down again. 'Whatever it was, I wasn't prepared for it, but I can't deny it. I can't turn my back on it.' She frowned. 'At least, I don't want to turn my back on it. Yet.'

When she glanced at him, he wasn't laughing. He simply stared back in deadly earnest. 'You and Mitch always connected like that, Tash. Why should it surprise you now?'

'But…but that stuff that happened before was *eight years ago.*'

'Doesn't make it any less real.'

'I was just a kid.'

'You were more woman than child.'

Her mouth went dry.

'And it might've happened eight years ago, but as far as I can see it's still alive and kicking today. The heat the two of you gave off at the police station…' he shook his head '…it was smokin'.'

Oh, great. Just great. She leapt to her feet. 'We only spent four days together. It's just nonsense to think that any of it could be real.'

It wasn't possible to feel this deeply about someone in such a short amount of time. She paced back and forth in front of the coffee table. Truly, when you got down to it, how much time had they spent in each other's company—six weeks eight years ago and four days this week?

It was ludicrous. It couldn't be enough to turn her whole life upside down. 'Maybe it's just a lust hormone thing?'

'That's certainly a convenient excuse to hide behind.'

She swallowed slowly before lifting her head. 'He betrayed me, Rick. He used me.'

'Eight years ago he thought he was protecting you.' His lips twisted. 'Eight years ago he had trouble keeping his hands off you too. But he did. He's a good guy, Tash.'

She knew that too. She perched on the edge of the sofa. She eased back until she huddled against its arm.

'You haven't said what you're afraid of yet.'

She didn't want to say the words out loud. Not facing facts didn't help in the long run, though. She'd learned that lesson when she'd been eight years old. She hauled in a breath and hoped her voice would remain strong and steady. 'I'm afraid that Mitch and I are going to fall into some kind of hot and heavy relationship and…and that we'll end up tearing each other apart, destroying each other.' Like her mother and father. Like Mitch's mother and father.

'And yet you still don't want to walk away?'

She slumped. 'I have rocks in my head, right?'

'You don't want to walk away because you think there might be something worth exploring, but you don't want to tear out each other's hearts in the process either.' He shook his head. 'That's not crazy.'

He shifted, straightened a little. A rush of warmth filtered through her. Dear Rick. Always searching for the best solution to a problem.

'So what you want, then, is for Mitch to give the two of you a chance to see where things might go, to see how they might develop?'

'Oh, I'm pretty sure he's going to be all for taking things to the next level.'

'But…?'

'I just don't know how that's going to be possible. He doesn't trust me. He sure doesn't trust my judgement.'

'He just wants to keep you safe.'

She thought about his mother and had to close her eyes for a moment. 'He wants to put me in a cage and I couldn't stand it.'

'Then you have to make him see what it is you need to make you happy.'

Very slowly she nodded. That was *exactly* what she needed to do, but…would it make any difference? Would he see why she couldn't live the kind of life he wanted her to? Would he even listen to her?

The sympathy in Rick's eyes made her reach up to scratch between her shoulder blades. 'What?'

'Why are you hiding from the truth? Seems to me that won't help your cause.'

What truth? 'Go on,' she demanded although her voice came out small.

'Tash, you loved the guy eight years ago and you love him now. I'm not sure you ever stopped loving him.'

'But—'

'Even if you've buried it for years beneath a whole truck-load of hurt and anger.'

She stiffened. 'We haven't known each other long enough for love.'

'Says who? Perceived wisdom? Seems to me that love makes up its own rules—doesn't seem to be any logic to it whatsoever.'

Her heart leapt in recognition, the same way it had that day in the sea cave. Unconsciously, she fingered the shell she kept in the pocket of her shorts. Was Rick right? Did she love Mitch?

Her mouth dried. It was a crazy notion.

Rick gave a harsh laugh—a dissonant note in the soft-filtered early evening light that filled the living room. 'You want to know what's ironic about all of this? Even if Mitch decides he can live by your rules and the both of you do declare your undying love for each other, it doesn't guarantee that either one of you will be happy.'

Her heart turned into a lump of lead.

'Your father said he loved your mother but it didn't stop him from smacking her about. My mother claimed she loved my father—even if she wouldn't reveal his identity—but I can't see that brought her any happiness or joy. All throughout this godforsaken neighbourhood are tales of woe and heartbreak and—'

'This isn't helping, Rick!' She cut him off before he could depress her further. 'Love can't be all bleak and horrible.' She glared, hating what he said, even though at one level she knew it was true.

His head came up as if he'd forgotten an important point. 'You're right.' He grinned and it was a good grin. 'Remember the Schmidts?'

Tash grinned back at him. The Schmidts had been an older married couple who'd lived a street over from Tash when she'd been growing up. They'd been childless and she could see now that it had probably been a source of great sadness for them. Maybe that was why they'd encouraged the neighbourhood children to drop in for milk and cookies on a regular basis. 'Mrs Schmidt's Sachertorte was the best.'

'Don't try and make Sachertorte for tomorrow, Tash. Truly. It's complicated.'

Good advice. Though maybe Mitch could show her how to make it one day. If things worked out.

If.

She fiddled with an earring. 'Mrs Schmidt told me once that Mr Schmidt was the only man she'd ever been with. They married when she was eighteen and he was twenty-two. She said she was glad every day of her life that she'd married him. That was on their forty-fifth wedding anniversary.'

Rick stretched a leg out in front of him and stared at his foot. 'Mr Schmidt told me that the best part of his day was walking into his house after a day at work and seeing Mrs Schmidt.'

'*They* loved each other and *they* were happy. It works out for some people.'

So what was their secret? She glanced at Rick. 'Have you ever been in love?'

He shook his head.

'You don't want to, do you?'

'Seems more hassle than it's worth if you ask me.'

There was a lot of truth in that statement. But… She pulled in a breath. 'I think if you can make it work it might just be the biggest and best thing in life.'

'That's a big *if*, Tash.'

Her heart, that had started to lighten, grew heavy again. She nodded. It seemed an especially big *if* for her and Mitch.

He rose. 'I'm heading down to the cricket oval to watch the day-night game. I'm hoping to catch up with some of the guys. Wanna come?'

She shook her head. 'There're a few things I want to do around here. Have fun.'

Rick left and Tash stared around at the quietness of her living room and blew out a breath.

She supposed she at least knew what she wanted now. She wanted to find out if she and Mitch could be happy together.

She threw herself full length onto the sofa and rolled her eyes. 'Easy-peasy. Piece of cake.' Heaviness settled over her and she surged upright again and tried to shake it off. She grabbed her recipe book. First things first. She'd choose a cake to bake for tomorrow. Maybe once that was done she'd be up to tackling the harder issues.

In fact, she could make the cake today. She'd bought all sorts of exotic ingredients earlier. She could bake it today and ice it tomorrow.

She closed her eyes and opened the cookery book at a random page—cheating a bit by making sure she opened it at the easier, front part of the book—and stabbed a finger down. She opened her eyes and stared. Orange pound cake with lemon icing.

Fine. She'd make that then.

She collected the ingredients. She preheated the oven and greased her brand-new cake tin. She started creaming caster sugar and butter like there was no tomorrow. Her arm and the spot between her shoulder blades started to ache, but she didn't stop.

And that was when the idea came to her.

She sat, mixing bowl and all.

Mitch wanted to protect her from all evil— from anything that might hurt or harm her. That was impossible. He had to know that. It was just that he considered her lifestyle more dangerous than most. He thought her job put her in harm's way. What if she could show him, convince him, that she didn't need protecting? What if she could prove she was just as safe as the next person? She could *say* all of that until she was blue in the face, but he wouldn't believe her. But if he *saw* it in action...

Would that ease his mind? Would it allay his doubts and fears?

Could he be happy in a relationship with her then?

It was worth a shot, wasn't it?

She stood. She went back to creaming with vigour until the mixture was light and fluffy, until the pulse pounding in her throat and the hammering of her heart eased and she could breathe again.

CHAPTER NINE

TASH PACED THE length of the living room—back and forth, back and forth—and sent up a silent prayer that Rick, true to his word, had disappeared earlier this morning and wasn't about to emerge from the guest bedroom to witness her agitation. She should've heard him leave, but she hadn't fallen asleep until the birds had started to chirp. Which, of course, meant she'd then overslept.

She wiped her hands down her shorts and adjusted her shirt. Why hadn't she set a designated time for Mitch rather than that open-ended *mid-morning*? She glanced at the clock—ten-twenty-eight. That was mid-morning, wasn't it? Surely eleven o'clock became late morning. Didn't it?

She forced herself to still and glance around. She'd iced the cake. It looked pretty. She'd even put sprinkles on top. She'd washed the dishes.

The table was set with plates and napkins. Coffee was brewing in her brand-new coffee machine. Mitch had been right about that—freshly brewed coffee did taste better.

There was nothing left to do but wait.

Waiting had never bothered her before. She went back to pacing.

You've never fought for your heart's desire before either.

She twisted her hands together. Good point.

And then she heard his car pull up out the front and her heart tried to dash itself to pieces against her ribs. She patted her chest and talked it down off its ledge. She took a deep breath, and then another one. It brought a modicum of strength back to legs that had started to shake. She set off down the hallway at the same moment Mitch strode across the veranda. They stared at each other through the screen door. Devoured each other more like. When she reached it, she unlatched the door and pushed it open. 'Come in.'

'Thank you.'

He went to kiss her, but she stepped back.

His eyes narrowed. She swallowed. 'I don't want to cloud things by...'

'A kiss is going to cloud things? I'd have thought I'd have made them remarkably clear.'

For a moment she was tempted, seriously tempted, to do it his way—to fall into bed together now and talk later.

Oh, go on!

But then what else would she give in to? What else would she give up?

She took another step back. 'You said we needed to talk. So, fine, we'll talk. If you only came around here to—'

He pressed a finger to her lips. 'Don't say it,' he warned.

She stared at him and eventually nodded. She had to stop being so prickly if this conversation was going to go anywhere.

He removed his finger. 'I do want to talk.'

'Good.' She wiped her hands down her shorts. 'That's good.'

And then he swept her close and kissed her cheek. His heat hit her and his scent swamped her and just for a moment she forgot which way was up. And then he released her. Hauling in a breath, she shook herself, turned and led the way into the living room.

'I'd like you to ooh and ah appropriately.' She stalked over to the table and whisked the cover off the cake. 'Ta-da.'

He stared and one corner of his mouth twitched. 'You really made a cake?'

The beginning of that smile disappeared when he glanced around. She bit back a sigh. 'Yes, Rick is staying here, but he's out at the moment.'

He swung back and his eyes were too intense. She did what she could to ignore the judgement in them. She had to try and keep control of the conversation or they'd descend into an all-out brawl within seconds. She gestured to the cake. 'I bought a cookbook. It's an orange pound cake with lemon icing.'

Eventually he swallowed and nodded. 'It looks great. Very professional.'

They stared at each other for several long moments before she found the strength to kick herself back into action. She planted the cover back over the cake and moved to pour them both coffee. She set the mugs onto the table. Mercifully, without spilling them. 'I've been flicking through the cookbook and ANZAC biscuits don't look too hard. I might try those next week.'

She was babbling!

'Tash, I—'

'Sit and eat a piece of cake, Mitch!'

The words shot out of her like bullets. She couldn't—wouldn't—give him a chance to say something that would set her off.

He sat.

She cut and served the cake. 'I channelled Mrs Schmidt while I was making this.'

'Mrs…who?'

'Never mind.' She had to stop babbling. 'Can you make Sachertorte?'

'That's beyond my skill set.'

He lifted his piece of cake. She waited until he took a bite. His eyes widened. She took a bite then too and…

She sat back in her chair and grinned. 'It worked!'

He grinned back. 'You doubted it?'

'Sure I did. First I thought I'd accidentally used salt instead of sugar and then I thought I'd beat the mixture too much or not enough, or if I didn't burn it that it'd sink in the middle because I'd mixed up the measurements or something.' She sobered. 'It seems to me that a lot of things can go wrong in making a cake.'

He sobered too and she could see he knew she was referring to more than cake-making.

He pointed to the cake. 'But nothing did go wrong. You did everything perfectly. You are a baker extraordinaire.'

He took another bite, but he didn't smile. He put his cake down. 'Tash—'

'Eat your cake, Mitch!'

He stared at her. She stared back. He picked up his cake and kept eating. Eventually they both wiped their fingers on paper napkins and sipped their coffee.

Tash set her mug down first. 'I know what you came here to say today.'

He opened his mouth, but she held up a hand. 'I know you think we can sort out our problems, Mitch, that we can make *us* work, but I'm not so convinced.' He opened his mouth again. 'But,' she said.

He swallowed. 'But?'

'That doesn't mean I think there's no chance for us at all.'

His lips thinned. He sat back and folded his arms. 'That's big of you.'

Her hands clenched. Did he think this was easy for her? 'Are you deliberately trying to get a rise out of me…to start a fight?'

He dragged a hand down his face. 'No.' Then he pulled his hand away and his eyes blazed at her. 'But I do want you to admit that what we shared was more than just sex.'

Her mouth dried. She couldn't have said why, but it took all of her strength not to hunch her shoulders. 'It was more than sex,' she managed through a tight throat.

Something inside him unhitched—she saw it in the way his shoulders loosened and the way his spine now curved to his chair. And she couldn't have explained why either, but it made her ache.

Honesty. If you want this to work…

Her heart contracted to the size of the shell in her pocket. But she touched that shell and lifted her chin. 'I gave my virginity to you. It meant something.'

His head came up. A triumphant light lit his eyes—a possessive light—that made her heart thunder and brought all her fears rushing to the surface. 'But, Mitch, I can't live the way you want me to.'

'We can work that out!'

'Can we?' she shot right back at him. She refused to allow herself to be pacified by trite platitudes. 'My parents couldn't. Your parents couldn't. What makes you think we'll be any different?'

He sat back, pale. 'That was a low blow.'

Her eyes stung. 'It wasn't meant to be,' she whispered. His nostrils flared, but eventually he met her gaze again. She lifted one shoulder. 'I'm just stating facts.'

'Are you all doom and gloom or do you see some solution to all this?' he bit out.

'Testy, aren't you,' she sniped back.

'Too right I'm testy! If you would just let us do what comes naturally it'd do the exact opposite of "clouding things". It'd make them incredibly clear and simple.'

'Oh, really?' She folded her arms. 'Well, I don't happen to agree with you.'

He leaned in close. 'What's more,' he said, his voice low and delicious, 'I think I could convince you to give my approach a go.'

She had an awful feeling he'd be able to convince her all too easily on that head, but…

This was too important for them to screw up!

'What makes you think you know better than me?'

He blinked.

She slapped a hand to her chest. 'What makes you think you know better than me about what's right for me?'

He eased back.

'For argument's sake,' she continued, 'let's say we do make love with each other right here, right now.'

Her heart nearly failed her when he licked his lips.

'But once we're done—'

'And sated.'

She had to close her eyes and count to three. 'Are you then going to be happy for me to continue living in this house and working at the Royal Oak and living my life the way I see fit? Or will you expect me to give all of those things up just to give you peace of mind?'

He stared at her as if he didn't know what to say. And then his face darkened. 'Are you determined to destroy us before we get a chance to develop any kind of relationship at all?'

'I'm not trying to destroy us! It's what I want to prevent!' The words left her at a shout. She leapt out of her chair and wheeled away. 'I'm trying to find out if we can work! I'm trying to figure out if we can be happy together or if we'll end up shredding each other to pieces.' She swung back. 'And all you're interested in is—'

He shot to his feet too. 'Sorry, I—'

He closed his eyes and dragged in a breath. She ached to go to him, to wrap her arms around his waist and rest her head on his shoulder.

'I didn't mean to keep harping on an old theme, but...but I thought you were going to pull the plug on us before we got the first chance. I thought if I could keep reminding you about how amazing we were together...'

It wasn't something she was likely to forget. Ever.

'Tash, I... We're on the same page. I swear.'

She let out a breath she hadn't known that she was holding. 'Okay, then.'

He stared at her a bit longer and eventually nodded. 'You have a plan?'

'Sort of. I was hoping you'd give me today.' She narrowed her eyes. 'But I want you to be open to the things I'm going to show you.'

He adjusted his stance. 'What are you going to show me?'

She was going to show him her life. 'I'm not giving you an itinerary of the day, Mr Control Freak.' She folded her arms. 'You'll find out, and in the meantime you'll just have to trust me.'

He grinned then and her blood chugged. 'Done.'

'Okay, good.' She moistened her lips and then realised the hungry way he surveyed them. A twist of something red and hot slid through her belly. Oh, dear Lord! She clapped her hands. 'Well, c'mon then. Time's a-wasting.' If she was going to keep her sanity and not kiss him they had to leave. Right now.

She all but threw their plates and mugs in the sink before grabbing her handbag and slipping it onto her shoulder. She gestured for him to follow her down the hall and out of the house. She locked the door and led him past their cars and down the street. 'We're walking,' she said somewhat unnecessarily, but it helped to ease the silence between them.

She remembered another time when they'd walked—into the forest surrounding his cabin—and how he'd taken her hand. He didn't take it now.

Then she remembered what had happened when they'd returned from that previous walk and thought it was probably just as well.

She gestured for them to cross at a set of traffic lights to the council park with its cenotaph, jacaranda trees and picnic tables.

'On our way through we're just going to stop for a moment to say hello to the gents playing chess.'

'They still do that?'

'Sure do. Mind you, some faces have changed over the years, but I guess that's to be expected.' It was a tradition for the half a dozen or so retired men in the area to meet in the park daily and play chess or dominoes. 'I think their wives shoo them out to stop them from getting underfoot.'

The men greeted her before she'd had a chance to so much as wave. There were shouts of 'Hello, lovely lady,' and offers of seats, which she declined. Demands were then made as to where she'd been for the last four days.

'Enjoying the sunshine on my holiday.'

'That's what your boss told us,' Mario said, beaming at her. 'We rang him to find out what had happened to you.'

She was aware of Mitch alternately tensing and shifting beside her. She glanced around the group. 'Where's Alfred?'

'Antoinette has him painting the kitchen.'

That made her laugh.

'Who's your young man?' Nigel asked.

She didn't bother trying to correct them. They'd think what they wanted to think. Besides, she very much hoped it'd prove true. 'This is my friend, Mitch King.'

She drew him forward and he shook hands with the men, deflecting their teasing with such good humour it made her realise all over again how good—on every level—he must be at his job.

Wading in, she took his arm. 'Leave him be, gentlemen. We have to make tracks, but I'll see you all through the week.'

As soon as they'd taken a few paces she dropped his arm. It was too hard keeping a grip on her common sense when temptation and desire bombarded her. 'I hope you didn't mind that.

I knew they'd have been wondering about me.' She rolled her eyes. 'Even though I did tell them I was going on holiday over a week ago.'

He glanced down at her. 'So why do I get the feeling our just dropping by wasn't an accident?'

He wasn't stupid; she had to give him that. She sent him a wide-eyed stare. He shook his head and half-grinned. 'Nosy bunch, aren't they?'

'A bunch of mother hens,' she agreed. 'I call them the Neighbourhood Watch.'

'They wouldn't be real handy if a fight broke out or anything.'

'Perhaps not, but if they thought something looked fishy they'd call the cavalry. And sometimes that's enough.'

She could feel the burn of his gaze, but she didn't turn her head to meet it. She didn't want to drive her point home with so much force it set his teeth on edge.

'Next stop,' she announced, pointing.

Mitch glanced at the bland front of the community hall on the opposite side of the park and wondered what on earth Tash had lined up for him to *see* here.

They entered and he pulled off his sunglasses, blinking to adjust to the dim light. Spread out in front of them was multiple groups of twos on mats, taking part in some kind of martial arts exercise.

'Judo,' Tash told him.

Before he could say anything, he found himself bundled out of the way as four teenage girls surrounded her. Someone showed off a red ribbon and there were ear-splitting squeals and it was such a strange environment to see her in he found himself grinning.

Eventually Tash clapped her hands. 'Okay, girls, on your mats. Show me your latest routines.'

He straightened. She was their *trainer*?

With a smile, she pointed to a chair. It was far enough from the action that he wouldn't be in the way, but close enough for a perfect view of the girls...and their trainer.

'Don't take your eyes off your opponent, Lou. Casey, bend your front knee a bit more. Nice! Jo, I want you to show me the throw we practised last time.'

He sat there, amazed. Amazed that Tash had

such a rapport with these teenagers. And amazed that she had such a mastery of the discipline herself.

'She's one of my best students. You must be the friend she told me she was going to bring along. I'm Simon Fletcher. Are you interested in learning the art?'

Mitch rose and shook hands with the man who addressed him. 'Mitch King. Is this your place?'

Simon shrugged. 'I run this judo school, but we share the community hall with many other associates.'

Mitch turned back to Tash and nodded. 'She's good.'

'She'd have a real shot at the state title if she wanted.' Simon shrugged. 'But she doesn't want. You should come by and see her in action some time. Tuesday nights when she's not working.'

He made a note of that.

'Are you interested, Mitch?'

Oh, he was interested all right, but less in the sport and more in the woman.

'I might be,' he told the other man. 'I'm just considering my options at the moment.'

He knew what Tash was trying to tell him—

that her world was just as safe as his, that she didn't need a protector or a defender. His heart thumped. That was all well and good, but it didn't change the fact that she'd be safer in an office job and living in a nicer suburb. She'd be a whole lot safer if Bradford wasn't staying with her. But not even that thought could make him drag his gaze from her lithe, assured frame. And his heart kept right on thumping.

Tash set a schooner of beer in front of Mitch and set another for herself on the table before climbing up onto the stool beside him. 'I'm a bit peckish so I ordered some potato wedges with sour cream and sweet chilli sauce to share. If you're hungry I can order you a burger or a schnitzel or something.'

He shook his head. He didn't want to talk about food. He wanted to talk about her.

'It's been a long time since I've been in here.'

They were in the Royal Oak Hotel—Tash's pub. He'd stayed away for all these years because he'd known it was what Tash would've preferred. To tell the truth, it wasn't his kind of pub—distinctly blue-collar. Not that he had anything against blue-collar or the working classes, but he wasn't one of the workers from the nearby glass or automotive factories. Which made him a stranger here.

And if the swift covert glances cast his way were anything to go by, the clientele recognised it. Not that he felt threatened, just…on notice. Very interesting.

Tash wasn't a stranger, though. Just about every patron in this lunchtime crowd had greeted her as she'd ambled past them. He lifted his beer to his lips. 'Do you know every single person in here?'

She didn't even glance around, just lifted one shoulder and sipped her beer. 'Just about.'

'How long have you been teaching those girls judo?'

'Those girls in particular or teaching judo in general?'

He gazed at her blankly. There was so much he didn't know about this woman. He'd been treating her like the girl she'd been eight years ago instead of the woman she'd become.

And then he remembered making love to her and his skin grew so tight it almost cut off his blood flow. Mostly, he amended, shifting on his stool. He'd *mostly* been treating her as that young girl.

'Rick talked me into learning judo when I was fifteen.'

His gut clenched at the mention of the other man's name.

'He knew Simon and we came to an arrangement. I couldn't afford to pay for lessons, you see, but I'd come early and set up the mats and then I'd stay back afterwards to pack everything up, sweep the floor so it was clean for the next group to use the hall and that kind of thing.'

Rick might've been a good friend to her once, but Mitch still didn't trust him as far as he could throw him. Not that Rick would be able to do anything to Tash while the police were watching him so closely. It was the only thought that kept Mitch sane.

'Simon taught me how to avoid a blow, how to fall so as to do the least amount of damage to myself and eventually, when I was ready, how to fight.'

He stared at her. 'You don't like to fight?'

'No! Do you?'

Well, no, but…

'I hate violence, but knowing how to fight—not just to defend myself but to be able to disable someone else—that makes me feel powerful and I like that.'

He grinned. 'You're something, you know that?'

'One of the most useful things Simon taught me was to read an opponent's body language. That's been invaluable. Nine times out of ten I can prevent a brawl from happening in here before it starts.'

He didn't like the thought of her having to break up fights in here.

Their wedges arrived, golden and steaming, and Mitch's mouth watered as their scent hit him.

'By the time I was eighteen I'd progressed so far I started taking on classes myself. Those girls you saw today can't afford the full fees for the classes, but I don't charge Simon a fee for training them.'

The wedges and his grumbling tummy were suddenly forgotten. 'You're doing that for free?'

'Free?' She shook her head. 'I may not be earning any money from it, but it's not free. I'm giving back the way Simon gave to me. And, hopefully, down the track those girls will give back too. It's a responsibility, a duty that needs to be fulfilled, but it's not a chore. I enjoy it. I get a lot out of it.'

He could see that, but still… They both reached into the basket of wedges at the same time. He stopped short to let her go first, every atom aching with the need to touch her. He recalled the look on her face when she'd asked him, *What makes you think you know better than me*? and he forced the need down. When they made love again, he wanted her with him wholeheartedly. He didn't want her regretting it afterwards.

Clarke, her boss, came over before she'd had a chance to demolish said wedge. 'Don't even think about it,' she said before he'd opened his mouth. 'I am not jumping behind the bar for ten minutes while you duck out to do whatever urgent errand has just come up. I'm still on holidays.'

Clarke rolled his eyes at Mitch. 'See what I have to put up with? Anyone would think she's the boss and not me. I'm not going to ask you to work—not even for ten minutes—but I have to hire a new part-timer. Long story. I'll fill you in next week. But I think you know both of the people I've shortlisted…and as you'll have to work with whoever I hire I thought you might like some input.'

'Oh.'

'So I came over to ask if you had five minutes to glance over the applications or whether you're happy to trust my superior judgement.'

Tash rolled her eyes and then glanced at Mitch. 'Would you mind…?'

'Go for it.' He stretched one leg out. 'I'm going to order a burger. I'm starving. Want anything else?'

'No, thanks.' She grabbed another wedge and hopped down from the stool. 'I won't be long.'

He watched her amble over to the bar with Clarke, his eyes dwelling on the long length of tanned thigh visible beneath her shorts, and a sigh eased out of him. He snapped his attention back to the table, though, when he realised two men were taking the seats either side of him.

'I'm Pete,' said one, 'and this is Mick.'

Pete looked hard and wiry. No doubt from some kind of trade or labouring work. Mick was built like a rugby front row forward—gigantic.

Mitch straightened. 'Mitch,' he said. 'Nice to

meet you. Anything I can do for you gentlemen?'
He was determined to keep things pleasant. He
didn't want any trouble. He probably had a good
ten years on both of them. But there were two of
them. And this was Tash's pub.

'Tash has never brought a bloke into the pub before,' Pete said. He was obviously the spokesman.

'But she's a great mate of ours,' Mick said.

'And we just want to say that you better treat
her real nice and do right by her, if you know
what I mean.'

The hand Pete clapped to his shoulder held
an edge. Mitch stared at the two men, and then
glanced around the pub. Every patron in here
was watching them. A grin built inside him and
he turned back. 'I take it almost everyone else in
here feels the same way about Tash?'

'That's right.'

'I'm glad to hear it.' If anyone ever tried to
hurt Tash in here they'd have these guys to deal
with. And these guys would tear them apart. The
thought cheered him like nothing else. In fact, her
workplace suddenly took on a whole new sub-
stance. 'Tash is a great girl. The best.'

He stared across at her. She glanced around

as if she'd sensed his gaze, and then straightened and raised an eyebrow. He shook his head
to let her know he didn't need her intervention.
'I have no intention of doing anything but treating her right.'

Both men relaxed as if sensing his sincerity.
And he was sincere. He just wasn't sure what
treating her right best entailed.

'But I'm curious. Why are you guys so happy
to champion her?'

'She's one of us.' Mick raised a shoulder. 'Plus
she got my boy a job here at a time when…let's
just say at a good time. I'll always be grateful to
her for that.'

Teenage girls *and* boys? She obviously had a
wealth of hidden talents. Or maybe they weren't
so hidden and he just hadn't seen them before.

'She gave me some very good advice once,'
Pete said. He jerked his head at Mick. 'Your
shout, isn't it, mate?' Mick ambled off. Once he
was out of earshot Pete turned back to Mitch. 'I'd
been having a lot of problems with my foreman at
the glass factory.' He held his thumb and forefin-
ger up about a centimetre apart. 'I was this close

to losing it. Tash talked me down off a ledge and stopped me from doing something real stupid.'

Mitch could tell he meant something jail-time stupid, something that would've cast a shadow over the rest of his life.

'She got me an application form to work at one of the automotive factories instead and stood over me until I'd filled it out.' He leant back. 'They hired me and…' He spread his hands as if that said it all and Mitch thought it probably did.

Tash came back to the table then. 'Are you monstering my friend, Pete?' She slid onto her stool. She had a grace and ease that fascinated him. And a life that was starting to fascinate him just as much.

'Just making his acquaintance, my lovely.' He tipped his beer in their direction. 'I'll bid you adieu.'

Tash watched him leave and then turned back. 'Everything okay?'

For heaven's sake, she was a walking, talking community services advertisement and she didn't even know it. And he'd wanted her to quit this place so she'd be *safe*? Dammit! She did more real good in her job, it seemed, than he did in his. 'Yep.' His voice came out tight.

Her eyes narrowed, but she didn't challenge him. Instead, she said, 'I ordered a burger for you.'

'Thanks.'

And, bizarrely, given all the thoughts racing through his mind, the conversation moved on. They ate lunch, Tash told him funny stories about incidents that had happened at the pub and he found himself telling funny stories about his time in police training. They laughed. A lot. It reminded him of kayaking with her, of their fishing and snorkelling.

And making love.

He did his best not to dwell on that bit.

Eventually, though, the conversation petered out into a silence that started to itch. There were still too many things unsaid between them. Tash glanced at him and she lost the easy, casual grace she had earlier. Her hands twisted together and her face became tight and pinched.

He did that to her.

Him!

His chest started to cramp. *What makes you think you know better than me?*

'I had a talk with Rick yesterday about love.'

His head jerked up. His mouth went dry. She stopped worrying her hands to lean towards him with a frown. 'It seems very strange to me that something that should be so positive—a force for good and all that—can turn out so bad for some people.'

Like her parents. Like his parents.

'It seems that some people who claim to love each other can be happy together while others who claim the same only seem to destroy each other. I've been trying to work out why that happens.'

She paused, staring—glaring—at the table. 'You see, I do care about you, Mitch.'

Everything inside him froze.

'I don't know how much yet, but it's enough for me to not want to walk away from what we could have just because things have got tough. But, whatever this thing is between us, I don't want it to turn destructive. I know you have feelings for me too, but I don't want them becoming destructive either. I don't want us to be like our parents.'

His stomach started to churn.

'I haven't come to any real conclusions about the difference between good and bad relationships, but today I wanted to show you the things that make me happy, the things that I need in my life—my community, teaching judo, my job. Those things are all good for me. If you hate them, if you hold them in contempt or see them as bad influences then you and I are going to run into trouble. Big trouble.'

'I don't, Tash.' He knew enough now to understand that she wasn't trying to blow him off. He tried to force all of his own insecurities to one side. The way she had.

Honesty hadn't played a great part in their past. It was time for that to change. He pulled in a breath and met her gaze. 'Today has shown me what a shallow view I've had of your life. You do amazing work and you have good friends. I...I'm sorry I leapt to conclusions about all of that.'

She sat back and stared. 'Thank you,' she finally said.

Except...

He still didn't trust her current houseguest. Bradford mightn't be in jail, but that didn't make him innocent. Mitch didn't say that out loud, though, because he didn't want them to fight again.

Something in the set of her shoulders and the thrust of her chin eased. 'You can live with my way of life?'

'Easily.' As long as he didn't count Bradford in the equation.

She shuffled on her seat. 'So the question remains...'

He stiffened. 'What question?' He wanted all her questions answered so she could focus on them. He was falling for her so hard and fast it made him feel sick. 'I can promise you I will never ask you to change your job or where you live.'

She stared back at him and smiled. 'I believe you. That's not the question.'

It wasn't?

She leaned in towards him. 'Mitch, what do *you* need to be happy?'

Her. The answer came to him in a rush. All he needed was her. Instinct prevented him from saying the words out loud. They'd freak her out. Besides, he had no right to rush her. He swore then and there, though, that he would do everything in his power to make her happy. To make her feel loved and cherished and secure and anything else she needed. Forever.

He wouldn't rush her, but she was still sitting here at the table with him. She'd said she cared for him. He stretched out a leg and grinned at her.

She sat a little straighter, adjusted her shirt, but the telltale pulse at the base of her throat betrayed her. Heat immediately balled in his groin. 'I'd like you to see my house…where I live,' he said.

Her eyes speared to his.

'I want to see your face as you check out my kitchen. I have lots of newfangled appliances perfect for the hobby cook.'

Her lips twitched.

'I want to watch your face as you check out my music collection and my DVDs—to see if you can live with them.' If she couldn't he'd toss the lot.

She moistened her lips and it was all he could do not to reach across and kiss her.

'I really want to cook dinner for you tonight. I

want to watch a movie with you afterwards, listen to some music maybe, drink a little brandy.'

She swallowed. She rolled her shoulders. 'That sounds kinda nice.'

And while she was there he'd show her in every way he could that they were meant for each other. He'd convince her to stay the night. Whether in his bed or the spare one would be up to her.

Of course, if she stayed at his place for the night Bradford couldn't touch her. She'd be safe. Safe and loved as she should be.

And, if nothing else, he'd have the undeniable pleasure of waking up to her in the morning. The knot in his stomach loosened.

Tash stretched and sighed, feeling sated and sexy and warm to the very centre of herself. She opened her eyes and turned her head on the pillow to survey Mitch.

Her heart expanded until she thought it impossible for her chest to contain it. Last night had been amazing, incredible. A smile lit her up from the inside out. Maybe she and Mitch weren't doomed after all. Maybe, if they took things slow, they could make things work. She wanted that with everything she was because…

She loved him.

She bit her lip and gave a tiny shake of her head. She wasn't even going to think those words yet, let alone say them out loud. It was too soon.

Slow. They'd take things slow.

Mitch's eyes opened and the smile he sent her curled her toes. 'Morning, gorgeous.'

Her heart pounded. 'Right back at you.'

He leaned across and planted a kiss on her nose and pulled her in close against him. She snuggled against his chest, revelling in the feel of powerful male flesh beneath her hands and cheek.

He nibbled her ear. 'What do you have planned for today?'

Ah…

She eased back a little to stare down at him. 'I'm still on hols.'

'Excellent.'

She almost succumbed to the smile he sent her. She eased up to rest against the headboard, dragging the sheet with her. He eyed that sheet and a glint lit his eyes. Oh, how she wanted to succumb to that! But…

'But…' she said.

His gaze lifted to hers and she leant down to kiss his cheek to ease the sting her words might bring. 'But,' she repeated, 'I have a house guest I'm not going to neglect.'

He sobered. He eased up beside her and he didn't say anything, but the tight set of his shoulders and mouth told her all she needed to know.

She cleared her throat. 'If you don't have any plans today, I'd like…'

Those blue eyes searched hers. 'Yes?'

She pushed a strand of hair behind her ear. 'We very diligently avoided the topic of Rick yesterday.'

He eyed her carefully. 'I didn't want to fight.'

'Me neither. It's obvious you still don't trust him, though.'

He kept his mouth shut, which, she reflected, might be wise.

She turned to him more fully. 'I'd like you to get to know Rick.'

He blinked.

'So if you don't have other plans…'

'I don't have other plans.'

'Well, then, maybe you'd consider spending the day with him and me?'

He nodded. 'Okay.' But his face had shuttered closed.

Tash huffed out a breath. 'Yesterday surprised you, right?'

He lifted a shoulder. 'Sure it did.'

'Then can't you be open to the fact that Rick could surprise you too?'

His face darkened again. 'I don't doubt that for a moment.'

'Forget it.' She pushed out of bed.

His hand snaked out to capture her wrist. 'I said okay, all right?'

'No, it's not all right! You're determined to think the worst of him.'

'I want you to listen to me for a moment.'

She stilled at his serious tone. 'Go on.'

'I want you to stay away from him until this whole mess has been cleared up.'

She gaped at him. He couldn't be serious?

'After that I'll be happy to get to know him all you want.'

Rick was her best friend. He didn't deserve that from her. 'No!'

Mitch's jaw tightened and she pulled her hand from his. 'I'd trust Rick with my life. And, as you pointed out the other day—I am not an idiot. Why won't you take my word for it when I say Rick is not behind these crimes? Why won't you even consider it?'

'Because, from where I'm standing, Tash, I think your judgement on this subject is clouded.'

'Then that's your problem, not mine! And I take back my earlier invitation. I don't want to spend the day with you snarling and acting like an idiot kind of guard dog.'

She swung out of bed. 'I'm having a shower.'

When she returned to the bedroom, Mitch was still in bed—in exactly the same position as she'd left him. 'Can I see you tonight?' he asked the moment she met his eye.

She tucked her shirt into her shorts. 'I…no.' She slammed her hands to her hips. 'How on earth do you think this is going to work if you won't trust me…if you won't *listen* to me?'

He stiffened. 'You just need to give us time. We'll work it out.'

Would time really make any difference? The thought of having this same argument in ten years' time made her shoulders sag. She opened her mouth, but the phone rang. She gestured for him to answer it, grateful for the reprieve.

Whatever the caller said to him, though, galvanised him into immediate action. 'Right.' He hung up, leapt out of bed and started hauling on a pair of jeans. Tash did her best not to get distracted by the long, powerful lines of him.

He turned to her once he was dressed. 'Maybe we can finally put this behind us. Rick has just been arrested on assault charges. Assault against a woman.'

CHAPTER TEN

Assault against a woman? Rick?

Tash went cold all over. Couldn't Mitch see it? 'Someone is trying to set him up!'

'I don't want to disillusion or hurt you, Tash, but the sooner those scales fall from your eyes the better.'

He wouldn't even consider her position. Her jaw clenched. Doomed, that was what they were, and she couldn't believe she'd thought otherwise.

She didn't bother arguing with him. There wasn't any point. 'You're going to the station?'

'Yes.'

'I'd like to come with you.'

He shook his head. 'I'm dropping you home.'

Fine. She'd drive herself.

They didn't speak during the ten-minute drive to her house. He pulled out the front of it but left the engine running. With a twist of her lips, she pushed out of the car. 'I'll call you,' he said.

She bent down to stare into the car. 'Don't bother. You and me, Mitch, we're done.'

His face darkened.

She pushed up her chin, grateful that the cold anger stirring in the pit of her stomach gave her the strength not to curl up into a ball and cry. 'There's one thing you might like to think about, *Officer* King.'

He stared back at her, his face as hard and blunt as stone.

'Very soon you'll realise Rick isn't guilty of those crimes you've all pinned on him. When you do, will you kindly turn your mind to who might actually be responsible, because until they're caught I'm still in danger.'

He blinked. He opened his mouth. But then cynicism flashed across his face, chasing away anything softer that might've tried to raise its head. 'The sooner I can prove to you what a nasty piece of work Bradford is, the sooner we can put this nonsense behind us.'

Tash slammed the door and swung away. She didn't watch his car as it roared away. She stamped up the front steps and practically kicked the door open instead. Cursing, she flung her handbag into the bedroom, uncaring where it fell. In fact, she cursed all the way through the house. Coffee. She needed coffee—hot and strong. She filled the jug. She reached for a mug.

'Hello, Tash.'

Every hair on Tash's arms stood to rigid attention. Her scalp crawled as if with a thousand bull ants. Very slowly she turned.

Cheryl O'Hara sat in the easy chair opposite, legs crossed neatly and pointing a gun at Tash's chest. 'It's been a while.' She wore a ludicrously pleasant smile on her face.

Tash swallowed and nodded. 'That it has.'

But not long enough as far as Tash was concerned.

Tash suddenly had to fight an awful weariness and terrible sense of inevitability.

Mitch would kick her butt if she went wobbly now. That thought had her mentally shoving her shoulders back, though she was careful to keep her body language as unthreatening as possible. The jug boiled and clicked off. 'Coffee?'

'No, thank you. This isn't really a social call, Tash.'

'I realise that, but I've had a shocker of a morning. Do you mind if I make myself one?'

'Not at all. I expect we need the calm before the storm.'

Cheryl's words chilled her. She made the coffee. All the while she kept Cheryl in the corner of her eye, readying herself to take whatever action necessary if the other woman made a sudden move. Not that she was sure what action she could take. Cheryl had a gun, for heaven's sake.

'So?' Tash sipped coffee and feigned a moment of bliss. 'You're the one who's behind the violence and not Rick then?'

Cheryl's nostrils flared. 'The police are idiots.'

'You won't get any arguments from me on that head.' Oh, but one of them could make love like an angel. *I'm so sorry, Mitch.* Why hadn't she told him she loved him when she had the chance? It all suddenly became crystal-clear. She didn't care if they argued about the same thing every week from here to eternity. It'd be better than never seeing him again. *Idiot!* She'd been an idiot.

She curled her fingers around her mug and leant a hip against the kitchen bench. 'I should've realised earlier that you were responsible for all this.' She shook her head. 'It never occurred to me.'

She'd been too busy thinking about Mitch. And that might finally prove a fatal weakness after all. She pushed the thought away.

'You've been slow on the uptake.'

And now she was going to pay for it. She tried to strangle the fear that rose up to choke her. She had to keep a straight head if she hoped to get out of this unharmed. And alive.

She glanced at the gun balanced carelessly in Cheryl's hands and then frowned. She leaned across the bench to get a better look at it. Obligingly, Cheryl held it up so Tash could see.

'Cheryl, that's a slug gun.'

'Uh-huh.'

She frowned. 'You're going to kill me with a slug gun?' Getting shot with slug gun pellets would hurt like the blazes, but it wouldn't kill her. Not even at close range.

'Oh, no.' Cheryl sent her a beatific smile. 'I'm not going to kill you.'

Tash tried not to sag in relief.

'I'm just going to scar that pretty face of yours so much that no man will ever look at you again.'

And then she aimed the gun right at Tash's face.

Mitch pulled the car to a screeching halt five blocks from Tash's place. He sat, the engine idling, on the side of the road, drumming his fingers against the steering wheel.

Trust has never been a strong point between us, has it?

She could say that again.

Will you kindly turn your mind to who might actually be responsible, because until they're caught I'm still in danger.

He pushed back the wall of pain that surrounded him, his innate police training coming to the fore. Detective Glastonbury had told him they were ninety-five per cent certain Bradford was responsible for this spate of violence, and there was no denying that the evidence, while currently circumstantial, was compelling, but...

That still left five per cent room for error.

With a curse, Mitch turned the car around. Five per cent was the slimmest of possibilities, but it didn't change the fact that he should've escorted

Tash into the house to make sure everything was as it should be instead of roaring off in a jealous rage. A frustrated growl grated out of him. His professionalism had deserted him for the duration of this entire operation.

He pulled up two houses short of Tash's cottage. Nothing looked out of place. He ignored the front door to ease his way down the side of the house. He paused when he heard voices. Was Tash on the phone?

He listened hard and his lips thinned and every muscle he possessed tensed. There were definitely two voices. Of course, it could be a neighbour or a friend.

Five per cent? The probability was slim, but this time he wasn't taking any chances. He continued around to the back.

One glance at the lock on the back door and he bit back a curse. It had been jimmied. Whoever Tash's company might be, it was a fair bet that they weren't a friendly caller.

He glanced at the lock again. *Damn!* She had the flimsiest locks a man ever had the misfortune to lay eyes on. As soon as he had them out of this mess and Tash safe, he'd read her the riot act about those.

He crept through the back door and into a small sunroom at a crouch. He peered around the doorway and his blood ran cold. A woman had a gun pointed on Tash. A woman mostly with her back to him, and he had to quell every instinct to rush in there like an angry bull. It would only make things worse.

He eased back into the sunroom and flattened his back against the wall. He tried to still the pounding of his heart, to clear the red mist that threatened to descend around him.

Tash. Gun.

No way! No one was going to hurt Tash. *Breathe. Think!*

The banging of pots and pans interrupted him.

'What do you think you're doing?' the unknown woman screeched. He frowned. He knew that voice.

'I've had the worst day in the history of the world, Cheryl.'

Cheryl?

Cheryl O'Hara?

And a whole host of events suddenly straightened in his mind. *Rick wasn't the drug dealer.* He closed his eyes. The party had been at Cheryl's house. Traces of marijuana had been found on Cheryl. But Rick had said the drugs were his! *He knows more about friendship than you ever will.* Mitch cracked his eyes open again, his lips thinning. Why would Rick take the rap for Cheryl? Why would he want to protect her? What did she have on him and Tash?

'You're not shooting me until I've had breakfast.'

His shoulders tightened and his eyes narrowed. No one was shooting anyone.

He glanced around the door again to see Tash cracking eggs into a frying pan.

'It's barely ten o'clock, doll face. You haven't had time to have had a bad day yet.'

She dropped bread into the toaster. 'What's that—the wit and wisdom of Cheryl O'Hara?'

Jeez, Tash, don't make her angry!

But Cheryl only laughed. 'Uh-huh. So whose place did you stay at last night?'

Tash drove a savage spatula through eggs. 'Mitch King's. Remember him? *Officer* Mitchell King?'

The bread popped up in the toaster. Tash was chatting away as if…as if nothing was amiss. He admired her front, but…

But what? She was buying time, pure and simple.

'Girl, you still have a thing for him?'

She slid scrambled eggs onto toast. 'Looks that way.' She held up a plate. 'Want some?'

Nice idea, he applauded, but it didn't work. Cheryl slashed a hand in the air and the gun swayed dangerously. 'That guy ruined everything back then! I can't believe you!'

He gathered himself in preparation to launch himself at Cheryl. It wouldn't be ideal, but he wasn't giving her a chance to get a clear shot on the woman he loved.

He wished he'd told her that this morning—last night *and* this morning.

It would've sent Tash running for the hills.

He shook himself. He couldn't think about that now.

'Did you sleep with him?'

'Yep.'

The gun stopped swaying so erratically, the barrel pointing towards the ground, and he let out a breath. Best-case scenario would be if he could sneak into the room and get behind Cheryl's chair, where it'd be simple for him to disarm and immobilise her.

'You are such a loser. That guy played you like an idiot when we were in high school.'

'At least I wasn't stupid enough to be caught doing drugs.'

'I'm the one with the gun!'

He heard the sound of cutlery and watched in amazement when Tash lifted a mouthful of toast and egg to her mouth and ate. She met his gaze for a moment. He blinked. When had she realised he was there?

'I heard about your dad, Cheryl. I'm real sorry.'

Cheryl tossed her head. 'He was a miserable excuse for a human being.' Her hands shook. 'At least I'll never have to be Daddy's little friend again.'

Everything inside Mitch froze. *That* was why Rick and Tash had done everything in their power to protect Cheryl. Bile burned his throat. The people who should've protected Cheryl hadn't. It'd been left up to her friends to do what they could. And then he'd blundered in with his holier-than-thou attitude and—

Think about that later!

'So I take it you still have a thing for Rick?' Tash said.

'We're meant to be together! We're soulmates! And he'd realise that if only other women would leave him alone!'

He wanted to hug Tash for her presence of mind. Instead, he eased himself into the room and slid into the shadow of a bookcase and stood stock-still.

Cheryl started to turn, as if she sensed something. He flattened himself.

'Cheryl, if you hurt me I will make sure Rick never forgives you.'

Cheryl froze before swinging back to Tash.

'If you scar me, blind me, I'll make sure he feels so guilty that he stays here to look after me. If you hurt me in any way, I'll make sure you never have a chance with him. Ever. You hear me?'

Cheryl shot to her feet. 'He loves me, not you!'

Tash gave a surprisingly elegant shrug. 'I think I can convince him otherwise. I can remind him you're poor little Cheryl and that he shouldn't take advantage of you.'

'You bitch!'

'What kind of chance do you think you'll have with him then?'

That was when Mitch saw that Tash was weighing a stainless steel pepper grill in her hand and he remembered the way she could pitch a rock at a tin can on the beach, her deadly aim.

'I've changed my mind.' Cheryl's voice rose and shook.

He glanced at the pepper grill and then at Tash and nodded.

'I'm going to kill you and then I'm—'

Not going to happen. 'Now!' he hollered, bursting out from his hiding place.

Tash launched the pepper grill like a rocket and it hit Cheryl, who'd started to swing to face him, squarely in her right shoulder, knocking her off balance. The gun barrel lifted skywards. He leapt forward, snatched it from her hands before she knew what he was about, but not before she had the presence of mind to rake her nails down his face as she frantically fought to find his eyes. With a curse, he spun her around and shoved her face down onto the floor, one knee in the middle of her back. He slid the gun towards the back door and out of harm's way before grabbing one of Cheryl's arms and forcing it up behind her back. She cried out in pain. 'Be still,' he ordered.

Tash touched his shoulder. 'Don't hurt her, Mitch. She's not well.'

He eased his grip on Cheryl, but only a fraction. He snapped on handcuffs and then hauled her upright and sat her back in Tash's easy chair. He wanted to yell at her, tell her she was crazy, but she'd started to cry.

Really cry.

Tash shooed him aside and sat on the arm of the easy chair and wiped Cheryl's face with a tissue. 'Cheryl, why do you have to take things so far?'

Her empathy amazed him. A minute ago this woman had been pointing a gun at her!

'I have to have him,' she hiccupped.

'Even if it turns you into a scary bunny-boiler?'

More hiccups and a nod.

'Even if it makes you like your dad?'

Cheryl's sobs stopped, as if Tash's words had shocked them out of her. Her face pinched up so white Mitch winced.

'I'm not like him,' she whispered.

'What do you call it when you hurt people to get your own way? What do you call it when you try to force someone to love you?'

Cheryl shook her head wildly. 'No. No!'

Tash placed her hands either side of Cheryl's face and forced her to look at her. 'Rick loves you as a friend, but he will never love you more than that. It's time to face the truth and leave him alone, the way your daddy should've left you alone when you asked him to.'

Cheryl's face crumpled.

Mitch's heart clenched and his mind threatened to explode.

Tash touched his arm. 'Are you okay?'

He nodded. *But...*

Things could've ended so differently today. If they had, that would've been his fault. Tash could've been hurt. Or worse. A black darkness shuddered through him, descending over the brightness of the day. He rested his hands on his knees and concentrated on drawing breath into his lungs. 'Tash, your locks are terrible, you know that? You need to improve your home security.'

That didn't change the fact that he'd screwed up. Rick was innocent. Rick had always been innocent. Tash had tried to tell him, but he'd refused to listen.

The darkness pressed more deeply into him. He'd been so sure she was blinded by prejudice and a shared history and background. But that had been him.

He'd been so sure and it could've got her killed. Acid coated his tongue and burned his stomach. Trust. He'd refused to trust her. He'd betrayed her. Again.

Detective Glastonbury's team came and took Cheryl away. Mitch took one look at Tash's pallor and promised that the two of them would be along in a little while to give their statements.

He touched her arm. 'Are you okay?'

She started and glanced around. 'They're gone?'

He nodded.

'I don't know how on earth we're going to sort everything out, Mitch, but I love you.' She threw herself into his arms and clung to him. 'I've been trying to turn love into something rational and logical that I can control, but it's not like that, is it?'

He wrapped his arms about her and buried his face in her hair and breathed her in. 'No,' he agreed. 'Not rational or logical. But powerful.' Overwhelmingly powerful.

He couldn't believe he had her in his arms, and that she was safe.

Her arms tightened about him. 'When I saw Cheryl with that gun the first thought that came into my head was—I wish I'd told you I loved you.'

'I thought exactly the same thing.' He eased back to stare down into her face. 'I wanted to tell you I loved you yesterday…and last night…and this morning, but I was afraid it'd scare you off.'

She nodded. 'Nothing like a real scare to put that into perspective, huh?'

'Jeez, Tash!' He huffed out a breath. 'That's one way of putting it.'

She swallowed. 'It's just…I thought if we took things slow that…that we'd have a better chance of success.'

He eased out of her arms and swung away.

'Success?' He turned back. 'I screwed up, Tash. Big time! You could've been hurt. Or worse.'

'That wasn't your fault. You're not responsible for Cheryl's craziness. You came back to make sure I was safe, didn't you?'

'Yes, but—'

'We saved the day, didn't we?'

He stilled and a glimmer of light lit through him. 'We made a pretty good team.'

She nodded.

He moved back in close to her, touched her face. 'I'm sorry I didn't believe you about Rick. All I could think about was keeping you safe. Because if anything happened to you...'

He couldn't finish that sentence. She reached up and cupped his face in her hands. 'I am safe. Now. Thanks to you.'

He pulled in a breath. 'I promise you that I will personally see to it that Rick is cleared. Not just of these crimes, but the former drug charges too.'

'Thank you.'

'I can't believe I let myself be so blinded by prejudice.'

'I can't believe I let myself be so blinded by fear.'

He met her gaze again and her face grew even more serious. She released him to back up and perch on the sofa. 'I'm still scared,' she said. 'Not about Cheryl,' she added before he could reassure her. 'About us. We love each other, but can we make this work?'

He moved beside her and took her hand. 'I want it to work.'

'Me too.'

Wanting and making it happen, though, were two different things. 'We've both seen too much of the darker side of life to believe in fairy tales, haven't we?'

Tash nodded, but it didn't stop her from wanting that fairy tale with every fibre of her being.

'Okay—' he turned to face her more fully '—let's talk about deal breakers.'

She blinked. And then she saw the wisdom of that. 'Yes.' She nodded. 'We've skirted around the hard issues for too long.'

'You want to start?'

She pulled in a breath. 'That's what yesterday was about. Did you lie when you said you could live with the way I lead my life?'

'No. I had that all wrong. The life you lead is

valuable and important. You're right to be proud of it.'

She let out a long breath. 'Okay, your turn.'

He rubbed the back of his neck. 'My job is important to me.'

She already knew that.

'It's a vocation, not a job. Through it I feel as if I'm contributing to something bigger and better than me.'

'I don't have an issue with your job, Mitch.'

'Not even if I were to arrest one of the Royal Oak's regular patrons that you might be fond of?'

She was silent for a moment. 'It's happened before. All of the pub's patrons know the consequences of getting caught breaking the law. I hate it when someone takes that risk, but I can't control other people's actions any more than you can. You have a job to do. I understand it's not personal.'

Some of the tension eased out of his shoulders and she suddenly realised one of his unspoken fears. 'I would never try to use my influence with you to get you to turn a blind eye to something you shouldn't.'

He stared at her for a long moment. She didn't

feel the need to fidget or drop her gaze but held his steadily. Finally he nodded. 'I believe you.'

They both let out a breath.

'I know your community here is important to you, Tash, but what if I was transferred interstate?'

Ooh, okay. She sat back. She thought hard. 'As long as I could still work and continue with my judo or some other form of martial arts then I could live somewhere else. I'd want to come back to visit my friends sometimes, though, and I'd like to invite them to visit me.'

He leaned towards her. 'You'd relocate for me?'

She'd never felt more bared in her life. She opened her mouth to add disclaimers like: Not next week, but if we've been going out for twelve months and everything is going well, yada-yada-yada… But that was just obfuscation.

'Yes,' she whispered.

He stared at her as if she was the most amazing thing he had ever seen. And then he slumped back against the sofa. 'What am I talking about? If you didn't want to relocate, I wouldn't move. Full-stop. I…'

He broke off and his hands clenched. Behind

the brilliant blue of his eyes she could see his mind racing. Her mouth dried. 'Mitch?'

He turned to her. 'The secret about love that you've been searching for, Tash?' She leaned towards him. 'I think I just worked it out.'

'Spill,' she ordered.

'It's not going to sound all that romantic,' he warned.

'I don't give two hoots about romantic!' She just wanted truth, honesty…him!

'Respect,' he said.

'Respect.' She rolled the word around in her mouth, testing it.

He gave a firm nod. 'Respect.'

They stared at each other for another long moment. She shifted. 'Okay, let me make sure we're on the same page about that word. When you say respect I interpret it to mean taking into account a person's feelings, emotions, thoughts and beliefs and giving them due weight.'

He nodded.

'So…' She hesitated. She wasn't sure she should go there, but she didn't want anything off-limits in this conversation.

'So?' The warmth in his eyes urged her to continue.

'So if you came to me tomorrow and said you needed to take me to a safe place because there was a police investigation currently underway suggesting Rick was out to hurt me…'

He dragged a hand down his face. Her heart alternately ached and pounded.

'And if I said I didn't believe Rick would hurt me, then…' She bit her lip. 'Then we'd go out to your beach cabin.'

His head lifted.

'Because I understand an innocent citizen's safety is of paramount importance, but then—'

'But then I'd work with you to try and determine—at a distance—who might actually be responsible whilst hassling my colleagues endlessly to explore other avenues, which is what I should've done.'

Something hard inside her gave way. 'Which is what you would've done if there hadn't been so many lies and secrets between us. If I'd been completely honest with you about everything from the start you'd have acted differently.' She saw that clearly now.

'I've never been objective around you, Tash. I want to say it's how I'd have acted if I'd known the full story, but I can't guarantee it.'

'I can.' She felt the certainty bone-deep.

He blinked.

'Keeping me safe is important to you. You'd do whatever necessary to ensure that, but we won't make those same mistakes again.'

One side of his mouth finally hooked up and he nodded. 'I think you're right.'

'Respect...' she started slowly '...is me listening when you tell me my home security needs improving.'

'Respect is me fighting my desire to lock you up to keep you safe because I know you're a person who values her independence, makes a valuable contribution to society and has every right to live her life the way she chooses.'

She wanted to slide right onto his lap then and lose herself in kissing him.

Her skin tingled, her fingers ached and every cell in her body reached towards him. She all but threw herself off the sofa and backed up to perch on the breakfast bar away from him.

He frowned. 'Tash?'

Her heart thudded so hard she had to press a hand to her chest. She hadn't allowed herself to hope, but now it all came rushing to the fore. She could do nothing against the gush of hot and cold, the fluttering and freezing or the surging of her blood. 'Are you saying you promise to respect me?'

'Yes!' He glared and slammed to his feet. 'What are you doing all the way over there? Tash, *I love you!*' He bellowed the words and it struck her that the same craziness and pulsing had overtaken him too. 'I know promising to respect you isn't romantic. But it means I will always take your concerns, your welfare, your health and your wants seriously. My parents didn't respect each other. Your father didn't respect your mother. I figure if we respect each other we—'

He broke off. 'Are you crying?'

'No!' A sob broke from her throat. 'And you're wrong. It's the most wonderful and romantic thing I've ever heard.'

In two strides he was there, arms around her and insinuating his way between her thighs. He stared down at her. 'You mean that?'

She nodded.

'I love you and I want to give us a chance, Tash.'

'I love you and I want you to kiss me.'

He did. Thoroughly and in such an achingly sweet way it touched her soul even as it made her toes curl.

Eventually they broke apart, both breathing heavily. 'We'll take things slow,' he said. 'Just like you wanted us to.'

'Okay,' she whispered.

He frowned. 'What exactly does taking it slow mean?'

She smiled. She threw her head back and laughed out loud for the sheer joy of being able to do so. 'It means we're not moving in together for at least six months.'

He pursed his lips. 'Can there be sleepovers?'

'I'm counting on it.'

'Slow? Right. I won't ask you to marry me for twelve months then.'

'And once we're married I'd like to wait a year or so before we have kids.'

He grinned down at her. She grinned back, winding her arms around his neck. 'I want to savour each and every moment of our relationship.' Because she believed in it now—believed in them. Heart and soul. She and Mitch would make things work *because* they loved each other, *because* they wanted the best for each other.

'I want to savour every day I'm lucky enough to be with you.'

She touched his face, awed by how much she loved him…and at the love she saw reflected in his eyes. 'Mitch?'

He pressed a long lazy kiss to the side of her neck and she arched against him like a cat. 'Hmm…?'

She tried to remember how to breathe. 'When you do propose to me, could you do it at the cabin?'

He eased back to grin down at her. 'Whatever you want,' he promised, his lips descending to hers again.

She kissed him back, telling him in a language that needed no words that she already had everything she wanted.

* * * * *

Look for Rick's story in
THE REBEL AND THE HEIRESS
Coming soon!

Mills & Boon® Large Print

November 2014

CHRISTAKIS'S REBELLIOUS WIFE
Lynne Graham

AT NO MAN'S COMMAND
Melanie Milburne

CARRYING THE SHEIKH'S HEIR
Lynn Raye Harris

BOUND BY THE ITALIAN'S CONTRACT
Janette Kenny

DANTE'S UNEXPECTED LEGACY
Catherine George

A DEAL WITH DEMAKIS
Tara Pammi

THE ULTIMATE PLAYBOY
Maya Blake

HER IRRESISTIBLE PROTECTOR
Michelle Douglas

THE MAVERICK MILLIONAIRE
Alison Roberts

THE RETURN OF THE REBEL
Jennifer Faye

THE TYCOON AND THE WEDDING PLANNER
Kandy Shepherd

Mills & Boon® Large Print

December 2014

MILLS & BOON®

Why shop at millsandboon.co.uk?

Each year, thousands of romance readers find their perfect read at millsandboon.co.uk. That's because we're passionate about bringing you the very best romantic fiction. Here are some of the advantages of shopping at www.millsandboon.co.uk:

* **Get new books first**—you'll be able to buy your favourite books one month before they hit the shops

* **Get exclusive discounts**—you'll also be able to buy our specially created monthly collections, with up to 50% off the RRP

* **Find your favourite authors**—latest news, interviews and new releases for all your favourite authors and series on our website, plus ideas for what to try next

* **Join in**—once you've bought your favourite books, don't forget to register with us to rate, review and join in the discussions

Visit **www.millsandboon.co.uk**
for all this and more today!